The Best
of Friends

The Best of Friends

by Margaret I. Rostkowski

HARPER & ROW, PUBLISHERS, New York
Grand Rapids, Philadelphia, St. Louis, San Francisco,
London, Singapore, Sydney, Tokyo, Toronto

All my thanks to my friends
Becky Reimer
Dixie Gaisford
Don Durkee
Judee Stanley

The Best of Friends
Copyright © 1989 by Margaret I. Rostkowski
All rights reserved. No part of this book may be used or reproduced in any manner whatsoever without written permission except in the case of brief quotations embodied in critical articles and reviews. Printed in the United States of America. For information address Harper & Row Junior Books, 10 East 53rd Street, New York, N.Y. 10022.
Typography by Joyce Hopkins
1 2 3 4 5 6 7 8 9 10
First Edition

Library of Congress Cataloging-in-Publication Data
Rostkowski, Margaret I.
 The best of friends / by Margaret I. Rostkowski.
  p.   cm.
 Summary: Three very different teenagers, once close friends,
struggle to understand the changes in their relationships and the
turmoil around them as the Vietnam War encroaches on their lives.
 ISBN 0-06-025104-2 : $. — ISBN 0-06-025105-0 (lib. bdg.) : $
 [1. Friendship—Fiction.   2. Vietnamese Conflict, 1961–1975—
Public opinion—Fiction.]   I. Title.
PZ7.R7237Be 1989   88-33077
[Fic]—dc19   CIP
                                                        AC

To my students

Contents

CHAPTER ONE

Spring Hike

Every year when the snow turned to mud and the light crept into the valley before six A.M., Sarah decided it was time to see spring from the mountains behind the house, time to talk Dan and Will into a hike to the top of Malan's Peak, where they could look out through the high spring sky, clear of cloud, all the way across the Great Salt Lake to the mountains of Nevada.

They'd done it since they were old enough to hike alone, since Dad taught Dan how to avoid rattlesnakes and Sarah to know the difference between poison ivy and horsemint. They always waited for Will at the bottom of the trail, and when he had panted up the hill on his bike, they would head up through the sagebrush and scrub oak, the dogs escorting them joyfully.

And now the three of them met at the trailhead again:

1

mud smell where patches of snow still melted onto the trail, whispers and rustles from the bushes, the young green of willows bending over the stream out of Taylor's Canyon, cool air slipping around Sarah's cheeks and down the collar of her jacket. And when Will turned off the motor of the truck, silence pouring over them. Quiet world of wet and rock and mountains coming alive to the west. Like every morning of all the springs they had come here.

The same. Except this year Will had left his bike at home under a year's worth of dust and had driven the truck. Too far to ride, he'd said, and Sarah hadn't argued. They were all here. Enough to be happy about, she knew. It had been touch-and-go. Will had worked the grill at Peach Palace until midnight and hadn't thought he could get out of bed by six A.M. And Dan had said he had things to do today and didn't have time for a hike. They'd only come for her, they both said, because she'd insisted.

As if the last seven years didn't matter to them. As if they'd forgotten they were graduating in a month and leaving, and that this time next year she'd have no one to climb with her, no one to help her count the golden eagles that sometimes blazed up into the air from the pine trees lining the canyon, catching and holding the spring light like low-flying stars.

Dan paced in front of the trucks, watching her as she tried to load the camera. He sighed when the film slipped out of her fingers for the second time. "I don't know why you bother, Sar. Every picture you take is a disaster."

He chucked three rocks onto the water tanks, then turned around and pounded his fists lightly on the hood of the truck, setting up a hollow rhythm that made Countess and Buff prick up their ears. "Get a move on, Sar. I haven't got all day."

Will leaned against the door of the truck, ruffling Buff's ears. "Lay off, Dan. What's the hurry?"

Dan looked over at him, one hand shading his eyes against the brightening air. "Just three tests and ten calculus problems." He closed his eyes a minute. "And I could be jumping right now." He stretched both arms up, fingers wide, and grinned over his shoulder at Will. "Just wait, man. You make that parachute ride down one time and you'll know what I'm talking about."

"Don't bet on it."

"I am. It'll happen." Dan pounded the hood of the truck, then pulled himself up onto it. "You start the paper for Quinn yet?"

Will shook his head. "Nope. But I'm thinking about it." He turned around and grinned at Sarah. "Plenty of time. Right, Sar?"

"Yeah, I guess. Darn, this is so . . ." She bent over the camera, slipping the end of the film into the narrow slot in the spool.

"Need some help?" Will crouched beside her.

"No, I've almost got it. Sorry to take so long."

"No sweat."

"Dad said I couldn't get a shot of the eagles because they move too fast. But I want to try." She twisted the

3

dial on the camera, listening for the smooth passage of the film around the spool.

"This his camera?"

"Yeah, his old one. It's a really good one, but he says I should stick to pictures of the dogs." She stood up and adjusted the camera strap around her neck. "OK. I'm ready."

Dan slid off the hood and Will slammed the door.

"OK, so let's not waste the morning." Dan vaulted over the fence at the trailhead, the dogs barking at his feet. Over his shoulder he yelled to Will. "Come on, Spencer. Get the lead out."

Will turned and grinned at Sarah. "Drill sergeant." Then he sprinted after Dan, shouting, "You're on!"

Sarah stood a moment, watching them disappear into the scrub oak, listening to their insults and catcalls as they headed up the trail. She'd never catch them. But she jumped across a mud patch and onto the trail. She didn't see them again until she got to where the trail opened out for a view over the valley, where they waited long enough for her to get a drink from Dan's canteen and to catch one breath before they took off again. She didn't hurry, but sat on a rock a minute to rest and rebraid her hair.

"You want me to wait, Sar?" Will called back to her.

She shook her head. "No, I'm OK."

She could have stayed up with them, but she never saw the point of making the climb into a race the way Dan did. And, of course, he usually won. As she stood up and readjusted the camera strap, she wondered if Will let him win.

And then as she reached the top, the trees opened around her and she had to sit down a minute because the wideness of the sky made her dizzy. She closed her eyes, waiting for her stomach and hands and legs and heart to stop shaking. When she had calmed down and could breathe without gasping, she opened her eyes and saw Will spread-eagled on the rock, far back from the edge, eyes closed, chest heaving. And Dan sitting near the drop-off, arms hanging limply in front of him.

The only sound was her breathing and the clink of the dogs' tags as they snuffled around the boulders and scrub oak.

She stepped as close to the edge as she dared and looked down. Muddy trail, downtown, the high school, Will's truck, their house—all like perfect toys. Only the mountains to the west looked the same. She pushed her hair back and felt the breeze on her face. Maybe the eagles would come and perch on her hand and tell her about their winter in Mexico.

She found a flat rock to sit on and her breathing calmed. She was above the world, high with the birds. Nice to play at being a child again, even if at times it seemed they had left it all so far behind.

She looked at Dan and Will. Dad would say they both needed haircuts. Will's curls shaded his forehead and edged around his ears. Dan's hair fell straight to his collar.

Mom called them her blue-eyed boys. It fit. Will had been like part of the family for years.

Friends at school envied her for the easy way she and Will had with each other, the way he'd stop by her locker after school and tease her, the hours he spent at their house, eating Mom's cookies and watching TV. What they never understood was that it was Dan and Will, and Sarah only if she didn't get in the way. That's the way it had always been. But Will did smile at her when she came to sit by him in history class, and did little things to show he didn't mind having her around. Like waiting for her on the trail. She wished she'd taken him up on his offer to walk with her. Maybe on the way down.

"Hey, look." Dan was standing, boots edged out over the edge of the rock, pointing out over the valley.

"What?"

"A plane. It's circling. Must be jumpers."

She looked out over the valley. It was hard to see against the colors of the town and mountains. Then she saw the plane, already up, not high above the airfield west of town, but climbing, circling, tracing a spiral in the sky.

"Wish you were up there, Dan?" Will said from behind him.

Dan turned around and grinned at him. "Damn straight. Watching you get ready for your first jump."

Suddenly two dots fell from the plane and immediately exploded into blossoms of red and blue and white parachute. The plane circled and then released two more dots that opened and spread out across the morning, dotting the pale sky.

As she watched from the top of the mountain, Sarah felt a bubble of excitement in her throat, and she wondered if this was what Dan felt when he jumped beneath that cloud of parachute. Just as she turned to ask him, the sky to the south cracked open and a swarm of helicopters rose from the valley, from the Air Force base, three, then four and five, hovering, dipping noses to each other, ripping open the air around them. They rose higher, even with the parachutes, and for a minute Sarah was sure they would tear into the fragile jumpers, but the choppers veered out to the west, black insect bodies scrambling up into the morning air.

"Wow, they're noisy," Sarah yelled, shading her eyes as she tried to follow the choppers into the light. "What are they doing around here?"

"Must be training out at the base," said Dan. "On their way to Vietnam."

"Look at 'em go," Will said. The helicopters were now only black dots above the mountains.

Dan ran one hand through his hair. "Idiots."

Will looked at him. "What do you mean?"

"You know how many choppers get hit in Vietnam?" Dan said over his shoulder. "They're sitting ducks."

Will blew at the hair on his forehead. "Doesn't look any crazier than jumping out of an airplane."

"Yeah, well, at least I don't have five thousand Viet Cong shooting at me. That's the difference."

"Whatever you say." Will turned away from the view of the valley and the parachutes, shoving his hands into his jeans pockets.

Sarah looked over her shoulder at Will. Trust Dan to ruin things.

"Hey, you two, I want to take your picture," she said.

Dan looked around at her. "Why?"

She shrugged. "For posterity. Come on, stand together."

Dan waved at Will. "Over here."

"No." Will stood up. "That's too close to the edge."

"Chicken." Dan laughed. "It's not far. Just don't look down. Come on." He jerked his head in the direction of the cliff.

Sarah fumbled with the snap on the camera case, sorry she had brought it up. Will stood rigid, hands deep in his pockets, as he looked up at Dan balancing on the edge of the rock.

"Hey, Spencer, we don't have all morning."

Sarah watched as Will edged over the rocks toward Dan and stood below him, not looking at him or out across the valley, but straight at the camera.

She smiled at him, then motioned to Dan. "Come on, get down by Will. You're out of the picture."

Dan sighed and made a face, then jumped down from the rock to stand by Will, taller by half a head, hands on his hips, easy in his long-legged body, fine light hair draping his forehead almost to his glasses.

Will looked like he did so often: serious, almost sad.

For a minute Sarah wanted to make him smile, tell him one of her silly unfunny jokes that he always laughed at anyway, but decided not to.

"OK, you guys, ready?" Planting her feet wide apart, making sure she was steady, she looked up at them over the camera, then back through the viewfinder. "One, two . . ." and she clicked the shutter.

Before she had time to wind the film, Will scrambled over the rocks to where she stood. "Now let me take one of you two." He lifted the camera off her neck. "Where do you push?"

"Here. It's all set."

"Hey, don't tell Mom or she'll use it for a Christmas card." Dan laughed, back on his perch at the lip of the rock. "You know how she is."

Grabbing him by the elbow, Sarah pulled him down to stand by her. "I don't like being up so high any more than Will does."

"God, what a bunch of—"

To shut him up, Sarah held her hand in front of his face, fingers wide in the peace sign, just as Will pushed the shutter.

When Will lowered the camera, Dan grabbed it. "Now you two. Just like home movies. Everybody gets a turn." He got down on one knee, while Will stepped over the rocks toward Sarah.

"Hey, you guys," Dan called. "You look miserable. Look like you like each other a little bit."

"You don't ask much, do you, Dan?" said Will. Then

9

Sarah felt Will's arm slide around her shoulders and she stretched her arm around his waist. His red shirt felt warm under her hand, his belt tight against the muscles of his back, as she stood, almost leaning into him, not quite daring to.

"Hurry up, Dan! How hard can it be to take a picture?" she called.

"Cool it, this has to be perfect." Dan peered into the viewfinder, looked up at them, and grinned. "The two Mouseketeers. Minus their leader. Say cheese, guys." He snapped the shutter, then lowered the camera. "Should be perfect."

Before Sarah could move away, Will said, "Let's take one more." He kept his arm on her shoulder, so comfortable and warm against the cool breeze circling the rocks that she couldn't step away.

Dan squinted at them. "Of you two?"

"No, all three of us."

"Who's going to take it?"

"I know." Sarah reached for the camera. "Here, Dan, get in close. If we put our heads really close together, I'll . . . Here, you grab the other side, Will."

"Sar, you get in the middle . . ."

"No, Dan, you're tallest."

"What a weird idea."

"You think it'll work?"

"Yeah, someone at school did it. It'll be funny. Just don't move, anybody."

Dan in the middle, Sarah and Will each holding a

corner of the camera at arm's length, Sarah's finger on the shutter, no one breathing, all three wanting to laugh, holding on to one another, the shutter clicked.

"Done!" Dan shouted.

The air sang with his word, and the rocks in the canyon below them echoed it back to them through the morning.

CHAPTER TWO

Mr. Clean

Last November 11, his eighteenth birthday, Dan had been shaken awake at dawn by his father, who told him they were going out to the airfield. Before he was really awake, Dan was sitting in a classroom with three other guys learning about wind velocity and correct landing procedure. And after three hours of class they strapped him into a chute and pushed him out of an airplane. Ever since, if he wasn't jumping, he was thinking about it, dreaming himself into the open door of a plane, and into those seconds, those eternities, in the air.

At first the dreams had been nightmares, ones where he fell, loose and tumbling in the sky, head spinning hideously out of control. But, as the number of his jumps increased, tumbling became flying and his head sang, high on air and cloud. Seeing those jumpers this morning made him feel the wind through his fingers and hair and in his eyes and mouth. And then those damn choppers had ruined it, with their ugly whopping sound, their hard shiny metal.

When he'd said so, Will had gotten pissed off for some reason. On the way down the trail, when Dan tried to talk about jumping, Will wouldn't listen.

"They teach you everything you need to know before you jump—how to sit in the door of the plane, about wind drift, how to control the canopy. And you practice falling—how to roll so you won't bust an ankle or knee or something. It's a blast."

Will didn't even grunt an answer.

"But the jump is the best part—falling, all alone, without anybody around telling you what to do or how to do it. *You're* in control, man. All the way. Nothing like it!" Dan picked up a pebble and spun it up into the trees. "Doesn't it sound tempting? Floating through the sky like a god?"

"You lost me when you said falling. The very idea makes me want to puke."

Dan laughed. "Hey, it's great. Nothing to it."

But Will shook his head. "Anyway, it's too expensive. I can just see Mom if I told her I'd blown fifty bucks on a parachute jump. That's a week's check."

"Hey, man, it's your money." Dan stopped and bent over to tie his bootlaces. "You're the one sweating over the grill and pushing the mop."

13

"Yeah, it's my money," Will said, not stopping to wait for Dan.

Dan looked down the trail after his friend. Will didn't have money to spare for anything. So he'd have to find ways around that. Dad had given him his first jump. He could do the same for Will.

Sarah came around the trail behind him. "Where's Will?"

He shrugged. "Up ahead."

"Come on, let's go."

"What's the hurry all of a sudden?"

"I just realized what time it is. I told Kris I'd help her."

"Do what?"

"Why do you care?"

"Hey, just wondering what you and the peace freak had planned for today."

"We've got a booth at the student union on campus. We pass out literature and buttons and stuff. And she's not a freak."

"Nobody up there will listen to a couple of high school girls. Even if they are into total brotherhood and love and all."

"It's not funny. This is serious."

"Don't get so uptight. I know it's serious. Kris just acts like she's saving the world, that's all."

"Maybe she is." Sarah hurried a little to catch up with Will, who was waiting for them at the turnout.

"Do Dad and Mom know what you're doing?"

"Sort of."

"What does that mean?"

"Mom knows."

"But not Dad."

"No." She reached for the canteen.

"Figures." He looked at Will. "Can you imagine how much Roald Ulvang will like having *his* daughter pass out antiwar buttons on *his* campus?"

"Dad doesn't exactly hang around the union," said Sarah. "I figure I'm safe."

"You better hope so."

Sarah tossed her braid over her shoulder and whistled the dogs to her side. "You guys working today?"

"Yeah, at two," Will said.

"Come on by. I'll give you some stuff to read." She turned down the trail again. "Really makes you think."

"I just don't want to have to talk to Kris," said Dan. "She makes me nervous. She's so *sincere* about everything."

Will shook his head. "She's not so bad. Dresses kind of weird, but she's nice."

Sarah didn't say anything, but Dan could tell by the way she was walking, arms stiff at her sides, that she was mad.

"Hey, wouldn't she be a great date for the prom?" said Dan.

"Yeah, why don't you ask her?" Will laughed.

"Maybe I will. She could wear her hippie clothes, and with me in my tux—geez, we'd be a knockout."

*　　*　　*

15

One thirty on a Saturday afternoon. Terrible time to go to work. He'd only gotten half the calculus done, looked over his notes for the tests once. Always the same this time of year. Tests, papers, massive assignments—as if teachers wanted to make sure everyone was exhausted by the last day of school.

He'd never had trouble studying before. But since jumping had taken over his life, he resented the hours he spent studying, hours he wanted to spend at the airfield. But he studied harder if anything. He had to keep the 4.0. For the university. For the scholarship. For Dad.

He'd pushed it today as long as he could, and now if he didn't hustle he'd be late for work. And he knew being late was unforgivable.

Dan met Will in the parking lot at the college and they clocked in just at two, before they headed for the Wattell Classroom Extension to pick up their cleaning equipment and get to work.

As he opened the wide glass doors, Will looked at Dan and grinned. "Only four hours, twelve rooms, five johns, fifty-eight ashtrays, and thirty-two wastebaskets to go."

"Have we counted?" answered Dan.

"Damn straight!" they yelled in unison.

Of course they'd counted, to help pass the time and to keep the mind alive. Dan often wondered how his father could have done this kind of work for twenty-five years without going crazy. Of course, Roald Ulvang was more than a janitor. He was practically head of Buildings and Grounds, chief of all the maintenance crew, except for

16

one supervisor who lived behind a desk and a stack of papers. It was Dad they called when boilers blew, pipes froze, or basements flooded. And while the professors called the other B&G crew by first names, they all called Dad Mr. Ulvang.

Dad *was* impressive. Even if he was just a janitor at a community college, he still made you feel like maybe you should salute when you spoke to him. The fact that he was head of the local draft board might be one reason. The local John Wayne, making sure every young man did his patriotic duty, making sure Dan registered for the draft on the very day he turned eighteen, right after he took that first God-awful parachute jump. Dan wasn't sure which meant more to his father, watching him fall ten thousand feet through the air or seeing him sign up to die for God and country. Yes, sir, Dad was red, white, and blue to the core.

But it was more than that, Dan knew.

Ever since he was a kid, Dan had wanted to please his father, whether in school or at Scout camp or with chores at home. He'd go over everything not twice, but four times, trying to look at what he'd done with Dad's eyes, to fix that one thing Dad might find wrong. That's one reason he liked working with Will, who didn't complain when a job took longer than usual because Dan was nailing down the loose ends. Anybody else would have quit long ago, frustrated and bored with making things perfect.

Will unlocked the janitor's closet and rolled out the

supply cart, while Dan picked up brooms and mops. They did a quick check to see if everything was there, then leaned together over the cart.

"Watches synchronized?" Dan asked, checking his sweep second hand with the wall clock.

"Check," said Will.

"OK, let's move. We have a record to beat."

They headed down the hall to the first door. Boring classroom, used mostly for sociology lectures. While Will swept and lined up the desks in rows, Dan cleaned the board, set out fresh erasers, and checked for any graffiti on walls and desks. Nothing exciting. People too busy taking notes to doodle.

Dan helped Will line up the last row of desks before closing the door behind them.

"Time check?"

"Seven minutes, thirteen seconds."

"All right. We're cooking!"

By the time they'd done all but the last room, alternating jobs, moving around each other's work without having to speak, they were ahead of schedule by five minutes.

"Breaktime!" yelled Will. Grabbing an unopened can of cleanser out of the cart, he jogged down the hall, then turned and lobbed it over his shoulder to Dan. "Take it, man. Go for the goal."

Dan lunged to grab it, feinted once as Will tried to tackle him, ran into the classroom to his left. Will reached for him, and when he missed, followed him through the

18

door, shoving desks aside, skidding on the linoleum. Vaulting over the desk at the front of the room, Dan crouched behind it, tossing the can from hand to hand.

"Come on, buddy," he crooned. "Come and get it."

"Get out from behind there and I will." Will danced from foot to foot, faking left then right. Just as he stepped to the left, Dan dodged out from behind the desk and they collided, spun, and crashed into the wooden podium. Before either of them could grab it, it tipped and fell, the drawer opening and papers spilling onto the floor.

They stood, leaning against each other, breathing in frantic gasps, looking down at the mess at their feet.

"Oh, shit," said Dan, when he could speak. He looked at Will and they both cracked up. They stood, whooping, out of breath from the game and the laughter, shuffling and kicking until the papers were strewn around the front of the room.

"God, what a mess." Will squatted beside the podium, gathering the papers into a pile. "Do you think they were in order?"

"Well, they sure aren't now. Here, maybe I can figure out how they go." Dan leaned over and grabbed a handful of papers and shuffled through them.

A door slammed at the end of the hall. They looked at each other.

"Dan?"

His father's voice.

"Crap," muttered Dan. "Quick, shove them in." He

righted the podium and pulled the drawer open while Will tried to wedge in a pile of papers.

"What's going on?"

Dan looked up. His father stood in the doorway, staring down at them, tapping an envelope against his leg. "This room should be finished by now."

"Uh, yeah," Dan said, "we had a little accident." He stood up. Will was pulling the papers toward him, filling his arms with them and fitting them into the drawer. Dan stopped and picked up two from under a desk leg and handed them to Will, then ran his hands through his hair, facing his father.

"What are those?" Dan looked where his father was pointing, at the papers Will was trying to get out of sight.

Dan shrugged. "I don't know. They fell out of the podium when we were cleaning." He glanced at Will. "Don't worry, Dad. We'll take care of it."

"I don't worry. I expect it to be done right. Without any more accidents." Stress on the last word. He started to leave, but turned back and held out the envelope. "When you're through, I have something to show you."

Dan stared at the empty door a minute, then dashed to the corner, grabbed up the papers, and crammed them into the drawer before gathering up the erasers. Will got the broom from the hall and began to work down between the rows. Dan stopped a moment to look into the hall and saw his father come out of one of the rooms they'd cleaned, cross the hall, and go into another.

"You in trouble?" Will asked as he edged the mop between desk legs.

"Don't think so. Nah, he would have blown at this if he'd been mad." Dan picked up a rag and wiped the board until it gleamed blackly, even the corners, where chalk usually lay unnoticed.

He grabbed the wastebasket and headed out the door to empty it. He couldn't see his father, guessed he was around the corner. Dad didn't usually check up on them like this. Maybe someone had complained. Some senile professor had gotten chalk on his pants.

No, Dad said he had something to show him. And if he had been on a raid, he'd have put on his furious Viking face and would have nailed them to the wall for messing around. It was something else.

When Dan and Will finished, checked all the lights and doors, checked them twice with Dad standing there, watching, his long arms crossed in front of him, and when they'd put the cart and equipment back in the closet, the three of them left the building together. While his father double-checked the locks, Dan and Will looked out across the walkways at the girls studying on the lawn in front of the library. Whatever it was, he'd find out in a minute. God, he hoped he hadn't messed up somehow.

"This came," his father said, and Dan and Will turned around. He was holding out the envelope. "Your AP scores. Will can be the first to hear how you did. I didn't even show it to your mother."

21

Dan stared at his father. His AP scores? He was supposed to open them here, in front of everybody? Dan took the envelope and ran his fingers along the edge. He could hear the girls on the lawn laughing.

"Dad, can't this wait? I mean, Will doesn't care about . . ."

"But *I* do." Dad put one foot up on the ledge that circled the lawn, and crossed his arms on his knee. "Very much."

Yeah, right. Dan looked at his father, leaning so casually there, long fingers loose in front of him, hair light against the sun. But he wore that look, when he tightened his lips and stared out of those blue eyes that never seemed to blink.

Dan opened the envelope and slid out a sheet of paper. He scanned the letter and then he looked up at his father, who was busy lighting his pipe.

"Here." He handed the papers to his father.

"How'd you do?" Will asked

"Fives in history and English." Mr. Ulvang read from the paper. "Not bad."

Not bad. Hell.

Will whistled. "Wow. Five out of five."

"But why the four in calculus?" His father held out the paper.

Dan sucked in a breath. "I . . . I've always had trouble in calculus. I spend more time on that than anything else. And I get A's in class."

"This doesn't reflect that." Dad shook the paper.

"It's still good enough for the university. They give credit for anything above a three." Dan took another breath, tried to square his shoulders, but felt like something was squeezing his lungs.

"You're capable of getting fives in everything. It just takes application and discipline." Dad straightened and handed the paper to Dan. "I'm disappointed."

Dan took the paper. He looked at it a minute, then up at his father. "I'm not."

"You should be." And his father turned and headed up the hill toward the student union.

Will took the paper from Dan and read it. He shook his head. "God, you're amazing, Ulvang. You aced it."

"Yeah, tell that to him." Dan flung his hand up the hill toward his father's back.

"Don't let him get to you. He's probably real proud."

"Yeah. Wonderful how he shows it." Dan took the paper from Will, read it over again before he shoved it in his pocket. Taking another breath, he stepped back and kicked the nearest garbage can, kicked it spinning across the pavement into the wall.

CHAPTER THREE

Mr. Ice

They always got something to eat after work. Will wasn't sure what would happen after that little scene with Mr. Ulvang, but Dan headed up the hill like always, not saying anything, and stomped through the basement of the union and into the Crest Room. Geez, they were alike, Will thought as he followed Dan into the snack bar. From behind you'd have trouble telling them apart, except Mr. Ulvang was a little broader and his hair had a little gray. And both such a barrel of laughs when they were pissed about something.

By the time Will paid for his Coke, Dan had found a table and was slumped down in his seat, legs propped on the chair across from him. He didn't even seem to realize that the table next to him was full of girls, didn't seem to notice the looks they were giving him.

24

He was doing it to himself again, the way Will had seen him do every time his dad got on his case for something. Even when he'd done more than a normal person could expect, if his dad said he'd messed up, Dan believed it.

Will smiled at the girls as he sat down. At least *they* didn't ignore him. He looked back at Dan, tearing open his straw and taking a long pull on his drink.

"So, how many people on the planet do you think got two fives and a four?"

Dan glared at him.

"Jesus, Dan, lighten up. Can't you be happy with those scores? Do you realize most people don't even take one AP test, let alone calculus? And if they do, they just hope to pass with a three."

He sat back, watching Dan stir his drink. "Only reason I even know about the AP test is because I hang around with you. You don't have to worry about that kind of thing in bonehead English."

"I didn't study hard enough. I knew I should have gone over that calculus again, but . . ."

"Will you lay off? This is ridiculous! You're the smartest person at Wasatch High. And I'm including most of the teachers."

"Cut the crap. The point is, I didn't study hard enough on the calculus. I messed up."

"Messed up? All you *do* is study anymore. That and jump. How come you let your dad get to you like this?"

"You don't understand. You don't have to live with him."

25

"No, but I've spent plenty of time around him. And you always let him do a number on you. You just sit there and take it."

Dan glared at him. "Let's drop it, OK?"

"Anything you say."

Will rattled the ice in the bottom of his cup. This never made sense to him, no matter how many times he'd seen it happen. Had Mr. Ulvang planned this? Had he walked away knowing he'd turned Dan into a basket case?

Maybe he didn't even know. Dan always waited until his dad left to fall apart. And around school he played Mr. Ice, acting like he knew he was better than most people could ever hope to be, with that look he'd shoot at you that said you'd just proved you were an idiot.

Will knew that other look Dan could get. He'd seen it that first year of Scout camp, when everybody was trying to do the mile swim. Will had been swimming since he was three and had finished his first time out. But Dan . . . Back then he was tall for his age and stringy and he never could do more than half a mile. The Scout leader asked Will to look out for Dan, so every afternoon he'd sit on the side of the raft and watch Dan swim, back and forth, farther and farther, until sometimes he was so tired he couldn't get out of the water. And he'd have that look on his face. Cold, exhausted, half scared, half angry.

Finally, the second week, he did the mile, with only Will and the swim instructor watching. He never talked about it, didn't tell anyone, didn't go near the water again. He didn't even seem to be happy once it was over. They didn't know each other very well then, so Will didn't get it. Now he did. Dan wasn't doing the mile swim because *he* cared anything about it.

So let him get it out of his system. Will turned in his seat so he could see the girls. Man, they were fine. Maybe college would have its good points. Too bad he never wanted to open another book or listen to another lecture. The very idea of more school made him as sick as thinking about jumping out of an airplane.

Wonder if those girls would smile at him the way they were doing right now if he was the campus janitor. Doubtful.

Dan drained his cup and flipped it into the basket behind him, glancing at the girls for a second as he stood up. He was ready. This was another of those times. He'd talked himself down where only Will could hear and now he'd pick himself up and walk out of here like nothing ever fazed him.

CHAPTER FOUR

Peace Now

It had not been a good afternoon. Not like Sarah had expected when Kris asked her to help. Sarah had imagined she'd talk to a lot of guys, answer questions, give out so many buttons and leaflets they'd have to send out for more. She thought people would smile at them, maybe wave or flash peace signs, be glad to see them. She knew some people might be angry, might want to argue about the war. She could have handled that. She'd read the handouts and was ready.

She hadn't counted on being ignored.

When they got there at noon, the student union was a mess—litter from the Friday-night movie crowd, campaign posters for student body elections crooked on the cinder-block walls. Dad would be furious if he saw this— even though the union wasn't part of his territory.

Bullwinkle blared from the TV set in the corner. "Cartoons. Can you believe it?" Kris asked while she and Sarah dragged a table over near the door. "Look at those guys. They look hung over."

Sarah glanced at the four boys sprawled over couches and across tables. They mostly looked asleep, she thought.

She and Kris arranged their literature and buttons and hung the poster on the wall behind them—a poster Kris had done herself: streaky blue background, stick-on plastic daisies, and the words "Peace Now" in Day-Glo orange. It looked handmade and a little sad next to the movie posters and glossy campaign photos. But all that mattered was that people would know why they were here. They weren't selling anything.

They stood behind the table until it was clear they weren't going to be busy for a while, so Sarah found a folding chair and sat down. When she'd been on campus with Dad, she usually hadn't been in the union, and it was fun for a while to watch people—coming from classes loaded with books, meeting friends by the stairs to the snack bar. A few professors passed by dressed in jackets and ties despite the warm day.

Kris didn't stick out as much here on campus as she did at Wasatch High, but today even by college standards she was far out, wearing a tie-dyed T-shirt tucked into a long India print skirt with fringe at the bottom. Her huge hoop earrings dangled under the bandanna knotted around her head. And moccasins—with beads and fringe and bells. Altogether wild. Sarah wished she dared dress that way, instead of wearing jeans and a sweater. Kris had told her to dress up so people wouldn't be afraid to talk to them, so she'd worn a good sweater. But Kris . . . Wow. How'd she get out of the house?

After a while the union started to fill up, and a few people stopped at the table. A couple of guys looked at their material, and one or two even took some, but they shook their heads and hurried off when Kris asked if they had any questions. But other guys did stop to lean over the table, fingering the pamphlets, and it took Sarah a while to realize that they weren't listening to Kris, that they were laughing over their shoulders to their friends as she talked.

One guy slid a flyer off the table and crumpled it into a ball. Before Sarah could say anything he lobbed it into a nearby wastebasket. A group of his friends began to whistle and yell, "Two points. Two points."

One of the cartoon watchers sauntered by, picked up a button with the peace sign, looked at it, looked at the other guys, laughed, and tossed it back into the box.

"Life is more than cartoons, buster," Kris said, grabbing the box off the table and shaking it.

He reached into the box over Kris's arm, took another button, and while they watched, carefully pinned it on his rear end and walked away. The last straw was when a paper airplane landed on the table in front of them. Kris opened it up and showed it to Sarah. It was one of their flyers.

Kris heaved herself into her chair. "I give up." Then

she grinned at Sarah. "Oh, well, maybe someday . . ."

Sarah couldn't smile about it. The laughter got to her. Dad might make her furious when he talked about bombing North Vietnam, and Dan might sound as if he knew it all whenever he started to lecture about the background of the war, but it certainly wasn't anything anybody ever laughed about, for Pete's sake.

"Does this always happen?" she asked Kris.

"Yes, especially up here. Now, adults get mad, like you're being a bad little girl." Kris sat sideways on the table. "Last week, I went to a shopping center and tried to get people to sign this petition. You know what one woman said to me? 'I believe in democracy. I won't sign your petition.' " Kris raised her eyebrows. "Can you figure that one?" She sighed and fingered the buttons. "Maybe these guys don't want to think about the war. It's easier not to. Besides, they all have student deferments. It's not their problem. That's what a lot of them say. 'I'm not involved. Let someone else worry.' "

"I hadn't thought of that. That's the way Dan talks about it—all theory, like it was a thousand miles away from him."

"Well, it is," laughed Kris.

"You know what I mean."

"You'd think he'd see the problem," said Kris. "He's so big on history."

"Yeah, but this isn't history yet."

"I wish it was." Kris leaned toward Sarah. "But you know, even when they laugh at us, it doesn't scare me off. It makes me want to work even harder. To just show them that we're right." She sat back. "And sometimes you meet neat people."

As the day edged toward three o'clock, Sarah wondered where all the neat people were. No one had stopped to talk for at least an hour. She was kind of sorry she'd told Kris she'd stay until four thirty. She couldn't even read; it didn't seem right to sit here with a book as if she didn't care if anyone talked to them or not.

She wished she was as gutsy as Kris, who would go right up to people she didn't know, go up to groups of guys, and try to get them to come over to the table. Not many of them came, but she tried.

Sarah sighed and fiddled with her braid. "Face it, Sarah Ulvang," she muttered. "You're still little Miss Harriet High School." She tossed her braid over her shoulder and leaned her chin on her hand.

She'd been looking for Dan and Will, hoping they'd come by and break the monotony. But they were all the way up the steps from the snack bar before she recognized them. They were just two more guys in jeans and sweatshirts, two more people to walk by and either ignore her or laugh. When she saw who it was, she stood up and waved.

"You look glad to see us." Will laughed.

"I am. You're the first people I've known all day." She had an urge to reach across the table and hug him, dirty gray sweatshirt and all.

"Wow, save anything for us?" Dan asked, flipping

through the stack of peace packets on the table. "Have you given *anything* away?"

"Hey, don't knock it. At least we're doing something." Kris looked up at Dan, not smiling. "Not just talking about it."

"It's been kind of slow," Sarah said. "And kind of awful."

"Why awful?" asked Will.

"Oh, people didn't seem to care much." She fiddled with the buttons.

"They'll come back." Kris stood up and slapped a loose corner of the poster back on the wall. "It takes time to get people to think. Especially around here." She glared over her shoulder at Dan.

"Don't blame me. I just work here." Dan flipped his empty cup into the wastebasket near the door. "This isn't my problem."

Sarah didn't look at Kris. She could have died.

"Hey, Sar, want a Coke? I'm buying." Will jingled the change in his pocket.

"Oh, thanks. I'm dying of thirst. I'll come with you." She stood up. Right now she wanted to get out from behind that table more than anything. "Kris, can I get you . . . oh no." She sat down.

"What?" Will looked around.

"Oh, geez, look."

Headed right for them. No way to escape.

"What's all this?" He stood there, hands on his hips, eagle eyes looking right at the daisies.

Kris stood up, hands full of papers. "Here, why don't you take some of our literature? It tells the real story behind the war in Vietnam. Things you should know. And we have a petition—"

"Kris, this is my dad." Sarah pushed herself out of her chair and faced her father. "Hi, Dad. We're . . . *I'm* handing out information about the war." She hoped he didn't notice how her voice cracked on the last word. She took the papers from Kris, set them back down on the table. "*Against* the war," she said, a little louder.

"I see." Dad turned to Dan and Will. "And you two are helping?"

"No, just stopped by." Dan leaned against the table, pushing it a little against Sarah. She pushed it back.

"I see. And you say you have the real story about the war, young lady?" He picked up one of the pamphlets, flipped through it, then put it back on the table. "Well, I know the Pentagon and the President could use some of your wisdom. I take it you think you know more about all this than they do?" He flicked a cold smile at Kris, then turned to Sarah. "I assume your mother knows you're here, Sarah?"

It took a moment for her to answer.

"Yes." Out of the corner of her eye, she saw Kris and Will look at her.

"And you'll be home on time?"

"Yes." Face burning, she stared at her father. She would not look away.

He nodded and glanced up at the poster. "Be careful of the paint when that comes down." And he left.

No one said anything. After a minute, Sarah sat down and began to straighten the piles of papers on the table.

"Boy, I wish my father would be that cool," Kris said. "He'd kill me if he found me here."

"*Cool?*" Sarah choked as she said it, had to swallow hard. "He was insulting! He doesn't take us seriously enough to get mad. He didn't even bother to read anything. More worried about the paint on his precious walls!"

She stood up, still fussing with the papers. "And when was the last time Dad asked you when *you'd* be home, Dan? What a put-down!" She waved her arm and knocked the poster loose again. "Damn it!"

"I'll do it." Will stepped behind the table and pulled the poster free. "Give me the tape."

"God, Sar, don't get so upset. You didn't really expect him to read your little papers here, did you?" Dan waved his hand across the table. "He could have let you have it instead. You know how much fun that can be."

"He still absolutely infuriates me! Treating me like a . . . kid or something." She knew she was sounding like a kid, but she couldn't help it.

"Come on, don't get bent out of shape. You know how Dad is."

"Yes, I know how he is, but I don't have to like it, do I?" She looked at the three of them. "Do I?"

Dan shrugged. "No, but you gotta live with it." He turned away.

Sarah pushed her hair off her face. "Yes, unfortunately." She wished she could shrug it off the way Dan did. Mr. Cool. Nothing fazed him.

"Well, I gotta go," Dan said. He stood a minute longer watching Will and Sarah pull the old tape off the poster.

"Hey, Mr. Wonderful," Kris called. "Take some literature."

Sarah glanced at her brother as she ripped the tape off for Will. Dan looked uncomfortable, but shrugged and took what Kris offered anyway.

"OK. Sure you can spare it?" He grinned at Kris, then at Sarah. "You got to be tough, Sarah," he said lightly. "Don't let Dad hurt your feelings."

"I'm not worried about my feelings, Dan. I'm concerned about this." She shook one of the pamphlets. "I'm thinking about all the people over in Vietnam being blown up and burned with the napalm from American jets. Do you know that one hundred thousand Vietnamese are killed every year? Mostly by us? By Americans?"

"That's what happens in a war," Will said. "People get killed."

"A lot of the people we're killing are civilians." She turned toward him. "Not soldiers." She held out a pamphlet. "Read some of this."

Will shook his head. "No, I'll take your word for it."

"Since when did you get so fired up about the war?" Dan said.

36

Since she wasn't sure when. But what did that matter? She handed another piece of tape to Will. "Well, I am. Too bad you guys aren't."

"I'm taking some stuff." Dan looked at his watch. "I gotta go. Love to stay and save the world with you guys, but chemistry calls. Later, Will."

"OK," Will called over his shoulder.

"And Dan?" Sarah almost screamed at him, picking up a flyer and waving it at him. "Read it!"

She looked back at Will, handed him another circle of tape. "He won't read it."

Will grinned and shrugged. "Probably not. You can't tell Dan much that he doesn't already know. Besides, like he said, he just works here. Not his problem." He pressed the poster onto the wall.

"Well, what about you? Will you take some?"

He grinned at her, ignoring the paper in her hand, and touched her arm. "How about that Coke?"

He was being so nice, so calm, exactly what she needed. Instead of Dan telling her it could be worse. "OK." She took a breath. "All right if I leave now, Kris?"

"Sure, I'll handle the hordes." Kris tucked her hair behind the bandanna. "Thanks, Sar. It was fun. Will you help again?"

Sarah looked up at the funny little "Peace Now" poster and Kris standing next to it. "Sure. Why not?"

CHAPTER FIVE

History Class

Will slid into the desk and pushed his notebook and English book onto the rack under the seat. Looking around, he saw Dan and Sarah hadn't come in yet. He was early and had time to try to look at the chapter Mr. Quinn had assigned, the chapter he hadn't read, as usual.

He opened the book, trying to remember what page the chapter started on, or even what it was about. Sarah would have read it, would have notes to slide across the desk if he asked her. And Dan knew everything in the book already, probably knew it better than Quinn. And since he was teacher aide this period, he should be glad to help out. Will laughed to himself. Sure, help—after he yelled at Will for not doing the reading earlier.

His eye ran down the page of tiny print, over the map crisscrossed with dotted lines, the page where he'd found his notes from yesterday. He remembered Quinn talking about World War I and trench warfare. And the map said "Europe during World War I."

OK, so you found it. So now read.

But where was Sarah? She couldn't miss class today. He'd been looking forward to seeing her since Saturday, since he'd bought her the Coke and watched her laugh her way into forgetting the way her dad treated her.

He pulled the book closer. He couldn't sit here all day and think about Sarah laughing. He had to try to figure this stuff out. He couldn't afford an F on a quiz. Couldn't afford to flunk the class again if he was going to graduate. Bad enough being the only senior in a class full of juniors.

At the front of the room, Mr. Quinn stood writing on the board as the class filled in behind him. People stepped over Will's feet, said hi, opened books, and riffled notebook pages. Out of the corner of his eye, Will watched Karen Walters open her book and run her finger down the page. He leaned over until he could see the page number. For once he'd gotten it right. He looked back at his book. Man, he hoped Quinn wouldn't give a pop quiz.

Around him everyone quieted down as the teacher called the class to order, answered questions about the research paper, discussed last night's news. Will tried to focus, tried to pull something off the page into his mind. Even if Sarah did show up in time, he didn't want to use her notes today. He didn't like doing it, didn't want her to know he hadn't read the stuff, even though she never said anything, or told him it was easy if he'd just read it. But today, he didn't want her to know.

She'd changed this past year. She looked different, moved differently. He didn't know for sure when this had happened, but he knew the very second he'd noticed. It was in this class, about February. He'd come in a little late and she was already there, surrounded, totally, by guys, and she was talking, telling a story about something that happened in choir. And he noticed the way they were watching her and laughing with her on certain words and the way she put a piece of hair back and left her hand there a minute and the way she moved her eyes and how she reached out and touched Guy Jensen on the arm. He hadn't been able to sleep that night. And ever since then when he ran into her unexpectedly, he'd say something more stupid than usual. That's why he'd gotten here early today, rushed up from auto shop, so he could be in his seat, all cool, when he saw her.

But the minute Will walked in the door, he realized he'd forgotten the assignment, so he was back to square zero. Feeling like a jerk.

Karen Walters looked across the aisle and smiled at him. When he was in fifth grade, she'd told him that a group of fourth grade girls had voted him the sweetest boy in the school. Great. If you were a candy bar. He still felt like a jerk.

He looked back at the page. He'd lost his place. Damn, this stuff was boring. Who gave a . . .

He looked up. Quinn was calling names. He'd better

40

listen, figure out what was going on. He heard Benny Rodriquez say "Submarine warfare." Then Pam Wilson—"Espionage." Frank Crawford, right in front of him—"Battle of Britain."

He breathed in quickly. Oh, shit, the term paper. He didn't have a—

"William Spencer?"

"Uh, yeah."

Quinn walked across the room, grade book open in his hands, squinting down the row at Will, pacing like he always did in class. "Mr. Spencer, how is your paper progressing? Do you, by any chance, have a topic yet?"

"Um, yeah, I mean, I'm working on it."

"Let's hope so. The days are marching by, Will. D day is two weeks off. Having a topic would be such a help." The teacher turned to another student.

Will blew at the hair on his forehead and glanced at the empty desk to his right. At least she wasn't here yet.

He looked over his shoulder at the back of the room. Dan was there, sitting at Quinn's desk, taking the roll. When he saw Will looking at him, Dan raised his eyebrows and circled the air with his finger. So damn casual.

"Yeah, I know," Will muttered. "Get with it, Spencer."

He wondered if Dan was *ever* uncomfortable in a class, unsure of himself, ever worried that he wasn't going to make it. He'd never shown it. Will turned back to the front of the room, where Quinn was writing "Treaty of Versailles" on the board in huge letters.

41

Will flipped open his notebook and began to write, trying to pick up the thread of the lecture. Fourteen points, League of Nations, Italy, Germany.

"Keep it up, keep it up," he talked to himself. "Write: self-determination, lasting peace, Woodrow Wilson." Geez, he wished something would make sense somehow. Two weeks off, Quinn said. That close. He rubbed his nose. He'd never find a topic and get it done in time. No way. His pencil scribbled, writing the words he heard from the front of the room.

"Hey, Will." A whisper from across the aisle. He looked up. Sarah. Smiling at him. Holding up a photograph.

"Huh?" He frowned at her. "Where've you been?"

"Darkroom. Look." She tossed the picture onto his desk, pulled her notebook out of her bag, and opened it, still watching him.

The picture of the two of them, both squinting a little, both smiling, light bouncing off their hair, her shirt coming out of her jeans a little, arm on her hip as she grinned at the camera, his hand in front like he was reaching toward her.

"Like it?" she whispered, forehead wrinkling.

He nodded. "Yeah. Great."

She looked up at the board, then back at his notes. "What's he talking about?"

He shrugged. "End of the war. The big treaty."

"Borrow your notes?"

He nodded, handed them to her, not breathing for a minute while she read them over before handing them back to him. "Thanks," she whispered, then looked back to the front of the room.

He gnawed on his upper lip looking down at the words and scrawls on the page in front of him. This stuff didn't make sense to him and he wondered if it did to her. It sounded in his head like it looked on the page—a wad of black lines and numbers.

He looked at the picture tucked under his notebook. God, she looked good. And they looked good together. About the same height, her hair so straight, his so bunchy. Both looking like they were having a real good time together, like there was no place they'd rather be. He glanced at her and then bent over the page again, copying the names of countries that Quinn was writing on the board: Czechoslovakia, Yugoslavia, Bulgaria, Poland . . .

After writing the last name on the board, the teacher turned back to the class. "These countries were created by the treaty signed in Paris in 1919." He slapped the board with his hand, leaving the imprint of his fingers on the chalky surface. "Ripe and ready for Nazi takeover twenty years later."

He bounced the chalk in his hand. "Any questions?"

Books slammed shut, people pulled gym bags out from under desks.

"Yes, Frank?"

"You mentioned the effect of the war on domestic politics?"

Mr. Quinn nodded, and Will closed his notes. Good

old Frank. He'd keep Quinn going for the rest of class.

Sarah reached across to Will's notes. "Can I borrow them for a minute?" she whispered. "Get caught up." She made a face as she bent over his notebook, copying quickly.

He remembered Saturday, standing next to her, his arm around her, hers around him, in the warm morning. First time he'd gotten up the guts to do that, really be close to her. A lot different from the way they used to run and chase and tickle, like they did when they were kids.

The bell rang and the class erupted into sound and movement.

As Will glanced at Sarah, shutting his book, she slid his notebook on top. "The picture's great. Did the others come out?"

Sarah handed him a stack of photographs. "Take a look." She leaned on the desk and watched while he leafed through them: Dan and Will, Dan and Sarah, pictures of the trail and the creek and one of Will's truck.

The last one was the picture of the three of them. Will held it out at arm's length, looking around it at Sarah.

"Hey, it turned out. That's wild." He looked again at the three faces pressed together, faintly out of focus, slightly distorted, Dan's glasses crooked where they pressed against the side of Sarah's head, Will's hair low over his forehead, Sarah's face a little closer to the camera as she reached to press the shutter.

"Sar, that's your third tardy this quarter. Do you have

an excuse from the office?" Dan stood behind them, roll book in his hand.

"Look, I just developed these from the other day." Sarah took the prints from Will and handed them to her brother. "Aren't they great?"

Dan glanced at them, then back at her. "Where were you? You were fifteen minutes late."

"Geez, Dan, fifteen minutes! Don't make a federal case of it," said Will, gathering up his books.

"Right. Tell that to Quinn." Dan gestured to the front of the room, where the teacher was erasing the board. "I'm responsible for this stuff, federal case or not."

"OK, I was upstairs in the darkroom. I couldn't leave until the pictures were developed. Satisfied?" Sarah shuffled through the photographs and held the one of the three of them out to him. "Look at this one."

"They're great pictures, Sar," said Will.

"I can't let you off." Dan shut the roll book, not even looking at the picture. "Not without a note from a teacher. You know how Quinn is about tardies."

"Oh, bother Quinn." Sarah slid the photographs together. "So I'm late once in a while. He doesn't really care. And you don't have to be so uptight just because you're his aide." She picked up her books and walked down the aisle. "Mark me tardy. It's not the end of the world," she said over her shoulder.

Dan glared after her, wrote a big " T " in the book, then turned to put it on the teacher's desk and gather up his things. Will started out the back door after Sarah. He wanted to ask her for a copy of the picture if he could do it without feeling stupid.

"Mr. Spencer."

Will groaned. He wanted to avoid Quinn, didn't want to face any more questions about the paper. But he turned back into the class. "Yes, sir?"

"About the paper. You don't have a topic yet, do you?"

"Not exactly.".

He watched Mr. Quinn pull a rag out from the podium and run it along the chalk tray. "Look, why don't you get Dan to help you out? I know you two spend a lot of time together. Why don't you spend some of it talking about history? That's one of Dan's jobs as my aide, to help out people who need it." He pushed a pile of chalk dust into the wastebasket. "And you certainly qualify."

Will felt his hand tighten around the spine of the fat history book, felt it all the way up his arm and into his neck.

"What about it, Ulvang?" Mr. Quinn called to the back of the room. "Do you think you could help Spencer find a topic he could handle?"

Will wheeled and stared down the rows of desks at his friend. Dan nodded. "Sure, I've got plenty of ideas that would work out."

"Good." Mr. Quinn carefully shook out the rag over the basket, stepping back to avoid getting dust on his pants. "Will, your grade is shaky at this point. Very shaky." He looked up. "You know that, don't you?"

Will nodded. His head felt like it was in a clamp.

Dan came down the aisle toward them. "Sure, any time it's convenient. I've got a couple of ideas, stuff you'd like."

Did they expect him to say something? Will wondered. He couldn't think of anything that wouldn't sound stupid. He just wanted to get out of the room, away from Mr. Quinn, away from Dan, find Sarah.

He took a breath and pushed out "OK." He thought maybe he could go then, so he turned away and walked toward the door. He hoped he wasn't walking too fast.

CHAPTER SIX

Peach Palace

Dan slammed his locker door and kicked it when it didn't shut completely. "Christ," he muttered. "Everything's screwed up." He peered down the silent hall toward the stairs. Why did Will take off like that when Quinn was trying to talk to him, trying to pull his ass out of the fire?

Feeling in his back pocket for car keys, Dan started down the hall, past the janitor and his dust mop, for the stairs.

He sighed, feeling tired all over. Being Quinn's aide didn't give him time to study the way he'd planned. He spent a lot of the time worrying about Will, watching to see if he was taking notes, sweating through the tests when Will just sat and stared out the window.

Will had failed the class once. He couldn't do that again

and still graduate. But it seemed like Dan was the only one conscious of that fact. It never seemed to bother Will. That was the worst part. Will never seemed the slightest bit concerned that he might blow it.

Dan shook his head as he unlocked the car door, threw his books in the backseat, and got in. "Well, it matters to me, Spencer." He stared across the empty parking lot for a minute. Will had looked royally pissed when Quinn got after him, like he wanted to haul off and hit both of them. So let him be mad. It wouldn't be the first time. He'd get over it. No matter how mad he got, Will always stuck with him. And that counted for a lot.

Dan turned on the ignition and backed out of the parking space. He'd see Will tonight and ask him about the paper. He had to get going on it.

Dan's mood hadn't improved by the time he wheeled into the parking lot at Peach Palace to meet Sarah after that evening's choir practice. Ever since he'd seen his AP scores, he'd been really bummed. And then to have Will act like such an idiot today.

It didn't help that the place was jammed. Cars with jacked-up rear ends idled on the street in front, carhops swung from window to window, music from the three different stations in town blared from open car doors. When two guys in a VW finished flirting with Stacey Wilson and pulled out, he swung into their spot and pulled on the brake.

Before he could get out of the car, Stacey slid a number

under the windshield wiper and popped her gum at him. "Hiya, Dan."

"I'm going inside. Is Will working?"

"Yeah, he's on the grill." She turned away, tugging at her mini as she leaned into the next car.

Dan pushed open the door, nodded to the carhops, who all waved at him, as he straddled a stool at the counter. He saw Sarah in the back booth with a bunch of her friends.

"Hey, Spencer." Will looked up from the grill, pushed at his curls with the back of his arm, and nodded to Dan. "What's cooking?"

"You are."

It was an old joke and Dan felt his stomach loosen a little.

"Hey, aren't you due for a break?" he called over the jukebox.

Will set down the spatula and came around the grill, wiping his hands on his apron. "In a minute." He handed Dan a Coke. "We have been *busy*. Everybody's out tonight."

Dan glanced around at the crowded tables. "Yeah, looks like it. What is it, spring fever?"

"Whatever it is, I've got it." Will stretched over the counter and yelled above the racket of the jukebox. "Hey, Sar, that stuff'll give you zits!"

Dan glanced back at the table, wondering which one of Sarah's friends Will was trying to impress. He normally didn't come on to a group of girls like that. Dan took a swallow of Coke and the jolt of caffeine sparkled in his mouth, but didn't do much for his mood.

The door opened and five guys came in, sprawling across the counter, reaching into Levi's jacket pockets for packs of cigarettes and dimes for the jukebox. Two of them spun on the stools to check out the girls at the tables before sauntering back to say hi.

"Hey, everybody, only six weeks until graduation," yelled Mike Evans. "No more homework . . ."

They all took up the chant. "No more books, no more teachers' dirty looks."

"Oh, god, you guys, give me a break," said Dan.

"Hey, guys, look, it's Daniel Ulvang, all-American brain." Mike leaned across the counter so he could see Dan. "What's the matter, Ulvang, nothing to study? Or are you just slumming?" They all laughed. Mike looked around, grinning. "I know, Dan, you're really gonna miss old Wasatch High. But not me. They hand me that diploma, I'm gone."

"Uh-huh. You and Stacey?" someone asked, and they all looked toward the carhop window where Stacey was glaring in at Mike.

Mike shook his head. "Nope." He bit off the end of a straw wrapper and spit it out on the counter. "I'm getting out of town while I still can." He blew the wrapper in Stacey's direction, but it sailed only a few feet and Will caught it midair. "I'm not waiting to get drafted. Day after graduation, I'm joining the army." He straightened and flipped Will a backward salute. "Won't I fit right in?" He ran his hand over his crew cut.

Will laughed. "You thought PE was hard. Wait till you hit basic training."

"Hey, is Stacey really that bad?" someone else snorted.

"No, man, I really want to be in the army. Always have. Chance to see the world."

"Oh, sure, right. See Saigon and die."

"Come on! I'm really excited about this."

Through the laughter and cigarette smoke, Dan looked at Will as he leaned against the ice cream freezer, holding his glass in front of his grease-spotted apron, laughing with the others, teasing Mike about drill sergeants and jungle grass and Saigon bar girls. None of them knew what they were talking about.

"Mike, do you know how stupid you sound?" Dan said. The laughter subsided, billowed up and around, then quieted. "Enlisting to break up with someone is really dumb."

"Oh, excuse me. I know I haven't given it the deep study you have." Mike leaned forward again, peering around at Dan. "I guess when your dad's on the draft board, you don't have much to worry about, right?" Mike looked around at the other guys, grinning as they all laughed. He looked back at Dan. "I tell you what. You go to college and study history. And I'll go to 'Nam and study the bar girls." Everybody laughed again.

How would it be, Dan thought, to hang around cracking stale jokes and making a mess out of your life? To just let things happen, without planning for any of it?

He stood up and slid his fingers into his jeans pocket for a dime. "That's what's great about this war, Mike. America is sending Vietnam her best." Through their hoots of laughter, he walked back to the jukebox. Leaning one hand on the red-bubbled side, he ran his fingers down the list of songs.

Behind him, he heard Sarah laugh. He glanced over his shoulder, saw Mike and his friends now sitting at the booth next to hers. Will had come around and was sitting at the counter, the last seat, out of the way. Dan slid a dime into the slot and punched two buttons, and the jukebox began to glow and hum, its innards churning out a record, turning it flat, setting down the needle. Humming along as Jim Morrison's silky voice slid into "Crystal Ship," he walked back to straddle a stool next to Will.

He glanced at Will and took a breath. "Look, I wanted to talk to you about what happened today with Quinn. He doesn't want you to fail, that's all. That's why he tried to talk to you." He flipped a menu open, then shut it. "He's not hassling you just for the fun of it."

"Could have fooled me."

"What?"

"That whole class is a hassle for me. A waste of time." Dan could hardly hear Will's voice over the music.

Dan shifted on the stool. "But you need the credit to graduate."

"I know that."

Dan picked up the saltshaker, unscrewed the cap, ran his finger around the rim. What could he say? How could he shake Will up enough to get him going?

Will got up and walked behind the counter to refill his glass, before he turned around to face Dan. "You don't know what it's like to sit in that class every day. Nothing makes any sense—it's just a bunch of words. I spend the whole class praying he doesn't call on me."

Dan set the shaker down, not looking at Will.

"You said Quinn's worried about me? You know that paper?" Will leaned back against the sink. "I could work my tail off for the next two weeks on that thing, spend every waking minute in the library, and you know what I'd get? A C if I was lucky, and a lot of red ink all over the paper. 'Could have been better organized, Mr. Spencer. You forgot this big-deal point and that big-deal person.' " Turning away again, Will blew at his hair.

"I said I'd help you with it. Isn't—"

Will whirled around, fist clenched on the counter between them. "I don't *want* you to help me with it, Dan. I'd rather flunk."

"That's stupid. You flunk American history again, you won't graduate. Then where will you be? Might as well enlist along with Mike."

"There are worse things."

"Oh, that really *is* stupid. Don't say things you don't mean."

"Maybe I mean it. Did you think of that?"

Dan ran his hands through his hair. "What's eating you, Will?"

Will stared down at him for a minute. "I don't know. I just . . ." He stepped back to let one of the waitresses reach under the counter for glasses.

"What?"

Will turned to set his glass in the sink. He took a minute to push it under the suds, watching it disappear.

"Will . . ."

His back still to Dan, Will said something.

"What? I can't hear you."

"I said I'll do it." Will sighed. "Don't worry, I'll do it."

"OK, but you don't have much time." He pulled a piece of paper out of his pocket, unfolded it, and set it on the counter. "Here, I wrote down some things you might want to do the paper on. Just ideas to get you started."

Will picked up the paper and held it out in front of him for a minute. When he looked up at Dan, and they stared at one another, Dan was shocked at the anger on Will's face. It scared him, until Will's eyes changed and he shrugged.

"Don't sweat it," Will said, turning away.

Dan was about to ask what was wrong, then thought better of it. It was cool. Like he said, no sweat. He grinned up at Will. "How about some food? I'm starved. Fries and a malt."

"OK." Will tightened his apron and bent over the ice cream bins.

Dan watched him work for a minute, suddenly very hungry. He could taste the salt, feel the malt slipping cold down his throat.

"Hey, Will, we've got to think about the prom. It's two weeks away."

Over his shoulder, Will looked at him. "I've thought about it."

"Any ideas?"

"Yeah. You?"

Dan nodded. "How about Linda Collins?"

Will nodded. "She's OK. Kind of runs off at the mouth though."

Dan laughed, leaning back, pushing at the counter with both hands. "Well, it's not her conversation that turns me on. I just thought it'd be fun. You could take Kelly Henderson. We could double."

"Kelly Henderson? You've got to be kidding." Will turned on the malt machine. "She'd never go out with me."

"Uh-uh. Linda told me Kelly thinks you're really cute. Did you hear that, Spencer? *Cute*."

Will looked over his shoulder at Dan, grinning at him for the first time that night. "Yeah, sure."

"No, seriously. She said that. I think she'd go with you."

Will ran his finger along the counter. "Nah, I'm going to ask someone else." He started back toward the grill. "I'll get your fries."

"You're going to ask someone? Who?" Dan leaned across the counter. "Come on, man, tell me."

"You'll find out."

Dan started on the saltshaker again, watching Will work. Boy, at times Will scared him. You think you know someone for years, then they go off weird on you. They always double-dated. And Dan always set it up. Not that Will was hard to get dates for. All the girls thought he was cute—and sexy. He just never took the trouble. So, why now?

Obviously Will was still pissed about the paper. Well, even if things weren't back to normal, at least they'd talked about it.

Dan swiveled on the stool and leaned back, elbows against the counter, watching the crowd—Sarah, Mike, all of them. One thing he had in common with Mike was he couldn't wait for graduation either. Although he wasn't stupid enough to enlist.

Freedom. On his own at the university in Salt Lake City. Away from home for the first time. He couldn't wait. The sky's the limit. He started to laugh. Not even the sky. That he could sail right through.

CHAPTER SEVEN

Night in the Stacks

Will turned away from the librarian's desk. OK, Dan, he thought, here I am, in the library, with your precious list. So what do I do now?

He looked down it:

> Resistance Movement in France
> Vichy Government
> Lend-Lease Program
> Stalin and Hitler

Bunch of losers. Not just the last two guys, but the whole list. Nothing looked interesting. He didn't know what any of them were, except Stalin and Hitler. And who wanted to learn any more about either of them?

He wished he could just crumple the thing and heave it.

He blew at his hair and headed upstairs and to the back of the stacks where the librarian had pointed him. She said he'd find lots of books on World War II up there. Maybe something would spark his interest, give him an idea. All he knew was he didn't want to do any of the topics on the list. For a lot of reasons.

D day and counting, Dan kept saying.

Yeah, right.

940. The number he was looking for. He looked at the top shelves, reading the titles, watching for a familiar name.

940.3928. Battles, generals, more battles.

He took several books off the shelf and carried them to the nearest table. He glanced at the titles, opened one of them, and began flipping pages.

He told himself he'd work one hour before he took a break. It was hard to keep from looking at the clock. Finally he got up and sat in the seat across the table so he couldn't see the clock just by looking up. He twisted his fingers in his hair and bent over the book.

Someone scraped out the chair across from him, sat in it, pulled a pack of notecards from a folder, uncapped a pen. He watched out of the corner of his eye. He wouldn't look up, wouldn't pay attention . . . he looked up.

"Sarah!" He remembered to whisper just in time.

She waved to him, one quick off-the-shoulder flick of the hand, then got up again and went into the stacks behind her.

He watched her go, noticing her braid bounce on her

shoulder, her shirt coming out of her jeans, the beaded bracelet she always wore.

She came back with an armload of books and slid them onto the table. He pushed his books aside a little to make room.

"You using all those?"

"Yes." She made a face. "Isn't it the pits? What are you working on?" She picked up one of his books and looked at the spine.

"I don't know." He shook his head and handed her Dan's list. "Dan gave me these. What do you think?"

She scanned the paper, scratching the tip of her nose with her pen.

"Those are Dan-type topics, for sure. Not stuff you'd like." She took a rubber band off her stack of cards.

"Yeah, but I really ought to pick one of these."

"Why?"

Will looked away, trying to say this right. "Dan spends a lot of time helping me with stuff like this. And his ideas are always good. Better than mine would ever be."

"You don't know that."

"Yeah, I do. When it comes to stuff like this, Dan is always right." Will waved his hand at the books in front of him. "As a matter of fact, he's right about most things."

"Don't say that, Will. Don't let him run your life."

"He's not." Will grabbed the list from the table in front of Sarah and crumpled it up. "It's just that . . ." He stopped. Just that what?

"See, Sarah, Dan loves stuff like this. And he's good

at it. And I hate it. So what's the big deal if I let him help me? Who does it hurt?"

"You! It hurts you." Sarah pounded the table with her hand. She didn't seem aware that people around them were frowning, so he held a finger to his mouth, shushing her.

"I don't care," Sarah said, but more quietly. "Show him you can do the paper yourself, that you don't need his ideas, his old list." She grabbed the crumpled paper that lay between them and tossed it into the wastebasket by the bookcase.

"So now what do I do?"

"What would *you* like to do?"

He pushed at the books. What would he like to do? No one had asked him that. "I don't know." He shrugged. "Something about . . . oh . . . a battle, or guys who did brave things or . . . I got this one." He pulled out one book and showed it to her.

"*Heroes of World War Two*. Sounds good." She nodded and smiled at him. "So you *had* been thinking about choosing your own topic."

"Sar, I wish I could explain how it is to you." How do you explain something you don't understand yourself? "Dan is so . . . smart and in control and does everything so well. And I'm just this . . . jerk that he lets hang around."

"Will, I don't believe you."

"He does so much for me . . . helps me with school-work, got me the job at the college, fixes me up with girls. And what can I do to pay him back? Not a whole lot. The least I can do is shut up and take his help."

"You two are friends. People do things for friends without worrying about paying them back."

"I don't mean pay back exactly. I don't know." Will blew at his hair. "Like if I don't take his advice, I'm ungrateful, you know? Like I don't have any other way to do something for him."

"Except do your paper on the Lend-Lease Program?"

"Yeah." Will fiddled with the rubber band. "Kind of stupid, isn't it?"

"It sure is."

Sarah was frowning, with a look he'd never seen on her face before. He shouldn't have talked about this, shouldn't have said what he did about Dan. It wouldn't make any difference anyway.

"Look, how about Audie Murphy?" he said.

"For what?"

"My paper. He's that movie star who was a war hero." He pushed the book toward her, open to a photograph. "He was the most decorated soldier in the war. And now he's making westerns. Pretty cool, huh?"

"I guess." Sarah looked at the picture. Then she stood up. "Come on. Let's check him out in the card catalog."

He followed her to the front desk, watched her pull out the drawers, flip through the cards, enjoying himself for the first time ever in this library since he'd come in for Mrs. Peterson's reading hour when he was in kindergarten.

"Remember reading hour?" He leaned against the card catalog case so he could see Sarah's face. He wanted to be sure that look was gone, that she was smiling again.

She was frowning at first, but after a minute she said, "Sure." She grinned. "And those huge fish Mrs. P. had?"

Will hunched his shoulders and made fish movements with his mouth, waving his hands in front of him.

"Come on," she said. "Get serious." She jerked her head toward the checkout table. "They'll throw you out."

"Fine with me. That'd be a good excuse for Quinn. Golly, sir, I tried, but they wouldn't let me back in the library."

"Here." She reached out and pulled him toward her. "Here he is."

They bent over the drawer together as she clicked the cards by, one by one. He hardly dared breathe, he was so close to her. He could smell—what was it?—cinnamon. Why would Sarah smell like cinnamon?

"What do you think?" She looked at him and he could have counted the freckles on her nose if they'd stood there long enough, he was that close.

"Um, you . . ." He blinked. "Sure, looks fine."

"Great." She stepped aside. "Write it down."

"Write what down?"

She frowned at him. "The books. Their call numbers. So you can find them."

He didn't move for a minute, not caring for now that she was realizing how really lost he was, just wanting to stand there with her and talk and laugh and wonder why she smelled like cinnamon.

But she left, whispering over her shoulder, "See you upstairs." He copied as quickly as he could, everything on the card. He knew the numbers were important, but wasn't sure which ones, so he wrote down all of them. After he wrote down all the stuff for the four cards with Audie Murphy's name at the top, he looked at the cards in front and behind, not wanting to miss any.

"OK, Spencer, you're this far. Now what?" He wanted to race up the stairs, find Sarah, and ask her what he should do next, but he made himself stop and think, try to imagine what she'd tell him, what would be the smart thing to do. He leaned against the card catalog, looking around. Right. Ask the librarian.

So he did, and she found him a magazine article and some news clippings.

"Wow, Spencer," he thought, as he climbed the stairs. "Maybe this isn't impossible." He grinned as he thought about the title of the book Audie Murphy had written, one of the three under his arm. *To Hell and Back*. Murphy must have been in Quinn's history class.

He started with that book, because it looked shortest. Besides, it made sense to find out what the guy was like.

Sarah was busy, writing, flipping pages, erasing, holding the wisps of her hair out of her eyes with one hand while she worked. Will leaned back at an angle so he could watch her without seeming to, without lifting his head from his book. Man, she was busy. She really knew how to do this.

By the time he'd read three chapters, sort of, it was eight thirty and the librarians were announcing closing time in fifteen minutes. Sarah dropped her pencil and stretched, then sat with her hands on top of her head, eyes closed. When she opened her eyes, she was looking at Will.

"How's it going?"

"OK." He shut the book. "He's cool. Did you know he was an orphan?"

She shook her head. "I don't know anything about him."

"He was. His parents were farm workers and died when he was a kid."

"Do you have enough for a paper?"

He riffled the pages, pulling his mouth to one side. "I don't know. I'm not sure how . . ."

Sarah rearranged the books on the table in front of her. "I could help you organize it if you want. You read the books and write down the notes, and I'll help you put it together, OK?" She waved her hand at her own books and cards. "I'm almost finished. And I wouldn't mind. Really."

He wondered why she didn't stop long enough for him to say yes, yes, yes. She acted like he would be doing her a favor.

Hardly.

Without talking about it, they packed their books and papers away and walked out of the library together.

"You got a ride home?" he asked her as the door shut behind them.

"I've got the car." She nodded toward the parking lot.

"Did your dad ever say anything to you about being in the student union?"

She stopped, balancing her books on the railing in front of the library, and shook her head. "No, he's probably forgotten all about it. Dad's funny like that. If it had been Dan handing out buttons, he would have come unglued. He lets me get away with things."

"Why?"

"I don't know. Maybe he doesn't think my time is as important as Dan's."

In all the years he'd known her, Will had never known Sarah to feel sorry for herself. She wasn't now—she was just telling the truth.

"He'd have said Dan was wasting his time, should have been studying." She shifted the books to the other arm. "He really wants Dan to do well in school."

"Yeah, I know. Dan worries about that. Although why he should . . . he's such a brain."

"But you know," she said, looking out over the dark parking lot, "I kind of worry about Dan. He doesn't have a lot of fun. Not like in junior high, even last year, when you guys were always tooling off to the canyon or the pool on your bikes. He's such a grind nowadays."

Will waited as a group of people came out of the library and went down the steps past them. Cars started up in the parking lot and lights swept the dark lawn in front of them.

"He goes jumping."

"You know why he's doing that, don't you?" Will could barely shake his head before she went on. "Dad wants him to. Dad trained to be a paratrooper in Korea, but he never got to jump because the war ended. So now he wants Dan to do it. Like they're proving something."

"Well, they are. Proving they can do it."

"It's pretty stupid, if you ask me. Who cares if you're brave enough to jump out of some plane?"

Will let out a breath. Yeah, who cares?

"Do you think he really enjoys doing it?" Sarah asked. "I know he talks like he really loves it, but sometimes I wonder."

"Dan is never real easy to figure out. One thing's certain, he's sure hard on himself."

Sarah hitched her books to the other arm. "See, Will, that's what you do best of all for Dan. You take him as he is, even though he's totally obnoxious, and a royal pain." She looked so serious, like it really mattered to her that he knew this. He grinned at her as she went on. "Not a whole lot of people can put up with him. Including me, most of the time."

She stopped. "What's so funny?"

"You are. You're so serious."

67

"Well, I just want you to know that you're wrong about not being able to do anything for Dan. You stick by him. That's a lot."

"Yeah, maybe. I guess I just feel a little . . . I don't know. Kind of spooked about graduation and everything. I'll get over it."

Now she smiled across at him, where he leaned against the railing.

"You better get home and read about Audie."

"You sure you want to help me write a paper about a war hero? With the way you feel about Vietnam?" When she didn't answer for a minute and stood staring at him, he thought she was thinking it over, getting ready to back out on her offer.

But she shook her head. "No, that war was a long time ago. Now is what's important. And now is Mr. Quinn and this paper and . . ." She stopped and looked at him for a long minute again. "I gotta go."

She turned and jumped down the steps and left him standing there, still leaning against the railing, thinking of all the things he wouldn't get to say to her tonight.

CHAPTER EIGHT

The Hill

Dan drove into the driveway, pulled on the brake, and turned off the engine. He was trying to make his stack of books and notebooks into a manageable armful when he heard his father call his name.

"Yeah, Dad?" he shouted back.

"Out here!"

Dan stared up the hill a moment. What was it now?

"Out here" was the back plot, where Dad planted fall flowers every year, zinnias and chrysanthemums. As Dan headed over the grass toward his father, Countess and Buff hurtled themselves down the slope, growling joyfully. "Hi, boy. Hello, old girl." He stooped, pushed the big dogs out of his way. "Come on, get a move on." Dad hadn't looked up from the seed packets he was sorting. "Hi, Dad. You're home early."

"Afternoon off."

"Great." Dan kicked at a clod of dark earth.

"I talked to Dr. Steele today. He's head of the mathematics department at the college."

Dan took a breath. "Yeah?"

"I told him about your problem with calculus." He stepped over the packets of seeds, picked up the spade. Dan watched as his father worked down the rows, turning the clods, breaking into them and smoothing out the soil. "He said there's a class you could take this summer."

Dan stooped, picked up a lump of dirt, worked at it until it crumbled between his hands. His father stood with one foot on the spade, ready to push it into the ground, watching him. He had to answer.

"Dad, I appreciate your talking to him and everything, but I don't think I need to take a class. I mean, I'm handling it OK, it's just that I didn't do as well as . . ." His voice trailed off until finally he stopped, ran his hand through his hair, looked at his father, feeling his neck tighten, his stomach knot.

It seemed for a minute that his father hadn't heard. He pushed the shovel into the ground, bent over it, grunting as he lifted the dirt, turning it to the sun. When he looked up, Dan felt the urge to step back, but he didn't, willing his feet to stay planted.

"I don't call your performance on the Advanced Placement test 'handling things.'" Dad stepped over the furrows of dirt and picked up a seed packet. "I thought I had taught you to do the best it is in your power to do."

70

Dan sucked in his breath. "I meant . . ." He stepped forward, to the edge of the garden plot.

Dad sprinkled the seed down the furrows. "You're interested in history, so you've done a good job in it, but that's not the only thing you need to do well in. You need a strong math background, too." He looked up. "You know that."

"I *have* a good math background. Calculus is the third advanced class I've had. When I said I had trouble in it, I didn't exactly mean it. I just have to work harder in that class than in any other, that's all." Dan watched his father as he spoke, trying to gauge the effect of his words. "I did better on the test than anyone else in the class."

Crumpling the seed packet in his hand, his father looked up at him, the look from under the eyebrows that Dan hated. "Don't measure yourself against others." He tossed the packet to one side. "You start doing that and you'll end up with nothing but mediocrity. You set your own standards and work to meet those." He pointed his finger at Dan. "That is the only measure that means anything." He picked up the spade and started down another furrow.

"I do work hard."

"Not hard enough, apparently."

Dan turned away, feeling a wash of helplessness. Dad wasn't even listening.

"I want you to sign up for the class."

Dan wheeled, to stare at his father. "Dad, I don't want to go to school this summer. I need some time off before

I start in the fall. I wanted to work and earn some money and—"

"Enough!" his father roared. "I don't believe I'm hearing this!" He threw the spade to one side and stepped up out of the garden toward Dan. "You say you want to earn money instead of going to school? You'd throw away the chance to go to school so you can work to earn money to waste on God-knows-what?" Dad wiped his hands on a rag as he talked, scrubbing at his fingers without looking at them.

"Your mother and I work hard to give you this chance, Daniel Ulvang, a chance no one gave us, and I never want to hear you say you would rather work than go to school." He stood a foot away from Dan, and although Dan was almost as tall as his father, he still felt he was staring up at his father as he talked. "Do you hear me? *Never!* I gave up a lot so you could go to school without worrying where every dime was coming from. I did not do it so you could 'take some time off.' " He bit off the last words and stared at Dan before stepping back into the garden.

"You may be smart, but you still have a lot to learn. Do you understand me?"

Dan took a deep breath, staring at his father.

"Do you?"

"Yes." Dan's lips barely moved, and he felt he was forcing out the word. Then, before his father could say anything more, Dan turned and left.

Dan flung open the back door and stormed into the kitchen. He threw his keys onto the table, grabbed a glass

72

from the drainer, and reached into the refrigerator for the milk. Leaning against the counter, he drank a sip and then long swallows. His stomach curled at the first hit of the cold, then began to relax.

Taking the glass with him, he headed for his room, where he dropped his books on the desk, pulled off his jacket, and stood, staring at the wall as he drained the glass. Then he climbed onto his bed and fell asleep.

He awoke to the sound of the television and the smell of coffee. Rolling over, he looked at the clock. Almost five thirty. He had slept for over two hours. Rubbing his face, he got up.

When he opened the door, he heard the evening news. Walter Cronkite and the smell of coffee—together they meant evening. He stood at the door, looking down the hall to the lighted living room, where he could see the back of his father's head, see him lift his cup and drink, hear the rattle of the newspaper spread in front of him. More than anything, Dan wanted to get out of the house without facing his father. He knew Dad wouldn't bring up the subject again, but he couldn't look across a meal at those cool blue eyes leveling at him

"And in Vietnam today . . ."

Dan took a step down the hall. Every night, the same words followed by the same pictures. Guys in uniform jumping off or climbing onto helicopters, generals covered with ribbons standing with hands behind them, talking seriously to the camera, Vietnamese soldiers running through streets, hunched over their rifles. Or old women peering up at the camera from under their coolie hats, yammering something in that singsong language of theirs. Sometimes it was rows of body bags waiting to be loaded into airplanes.

Tonight the reporter was with a bunch of GIs in a helicopter heading God-knows-where. The guys were telling how they were going on a sweep of a village, looking for a VC cadre supposed to be in the area. As they talked, their fingers constantly moved over their weapons, touching bolts, checking the safety catches. Wind funneled through the belly of the helicopter, so they all had to shout to be heard. It all looked frantic, hyper, and on the edge of out-of-control.

He knew what it was to sit inside an airplane like that, to feel that mix of excitement and panic he saw on the faces of those GIs. And he was just jumping onto an airfield in Utah. What would it be like to land in a war zone?

The screen lightened into a Chevrolet commercial. Dan smelled hamburgers, heard Mom and Sarah talking in the kitchen. He grabbed a jacket from the back of his door, started out, then turned back. He reached up to the top shelf of his closet, pulled out a pack of cigarettes, and stuffed them into his pocket. He headed for the back door.

"Dan?"

Crap. He had wanted to get away without talking.

"I don't want any dinner, Mom." Over his shoulder.

"Honey, are you OK?" Mom stood in the door to the porch, spatula in her hand.

74

"I'm not hungry. I'm going to take the dogs out for a run."

"You sure?"

"Mom, I gotta—I'm sorry. I'm just not hungry." Before she could say more, he picked up the leashes, pulled on his jacket, and headed for the dog pen. Dad would tell her everything anyway, tonight when the house was dark. Later she'd try to explain his father to him, like she always did. Same old story that didn't make any difference anyway. He always ended up doing what his father wanted.

He could see Buff at the gate, his great tail sweeping the air behind him, the rumble in his throat ready to explode into excited barking. "Hello, old guy. Come on." As Dan bent to clip on the leash, he felt Countess bump him from behind. "Wait a minute, girl. Wait your turn."

The two golden dogs pulled him through the gate and out toward the scrub oak. He kept the leashes on until they were well away from the house and up the slope of foothill toward Taylor's Canyon. The trail was muddy, but not enough to stop him or slow the dogs, just wet enough to make the earth curl up around his boots as he walked. The cool of the air wore a hard edge. It would be cold tonight. Dad would be out covering the baby tomato plants.

Dan turned to look back at the house, feeling the same tightness in his neck from that afternoon. "Damn tomatoes."

Buff trotted back to check on him, sweep him with his

tail, then trot away after new scents. Countess was off to the left, exploring. The ground began to rise, and Dan hiked between the sumac and sage, up past the metal grating where the creek went underground, past the turn-off to the old mine, the ground sliding away to the left. At the rock field, he skirted the smaller boulders until he reached Castle Rock, jutting up from the surrounding boulders.

He decided against climbing it, not sure he could find familiar fingerholds in the darkening day. He stepped onto the flat rock that stretched in front of it—Picnic Rock, Sarah called it—the spot where they'd come so many times. Once on top he shaded his eyes against the setting sun. He'd better check on the dogs or Countess would take off after a rabbit and Buff would roll in something dead. He found them, whistled them both a little closer, then stretched out on the rock, boots hanging over the edge. He lay a moment, eyes closed, feeling his body settle into the rock.

Getting cold. He sat up and unrolled his shirtsleeves, pulling them down to cover his arms. "Well, hotshot," he muttered, "thought you could think for yourself, didn't you? What an idiot. You should know by now."

Stretching, he reached into his jeans pocket for the cigarettes. Another thing Dad would kill him for. Something else in there. He pulled out a square of paper, opened it.

"OLD MEN ARE RUNNING YOUR LIVES!!!!!" Big block letters.

Dan blinked. "So what else is new," he muttered. He turned the paper over. Where did . . . oh, right, Sarah's stuff.

He tapped out a cigarette and lit it, went back to reading.

100,000 VIETNAMESE DRIVEN FROM THEIR
HOMES EVERY MONTH
1,000,000 VIETNAMESE CHILDREN WOUNDED
100,000 VIETNAMESE KILLED ANNUALLY
36,000 AMERICANS KILLED SINCE 1962
250,000 VIETNAMESE CHILDREN KILLED

THIS IS THE DIRTY LITTLE WAR NIXON
WANTS YOU TO JOIN

SAY *NO* TO THE WAR IN VIETNAM
SAY *NO* TO NAPALM AND BOMBS
SAY *NO* TO CONSCRIPTION
SAY *NO* TO THE OLD MEN
IN THE WHITE HOUSE AND PENTAGON
TAKE CONTROL OF YOUR DESTINY
JOIN YOUR BROTHERS AND SISTERS
HELP TO END THE WAR IN VIETNAM
BEFORE IT ENDS ALL OF US

Utah Coalition for Peace

Dan folded the paper back into its little square, then ground out the cigarette on the rock. He broke off a sprig of sagebrush and ran his fingers up it, crushing the fragrant gray leaves. He unfolded the paper again, read the first words again.

"Old men running your lives." So what was different about that?

He tossed the sagebrush onto the dirt in front of him, plucked another branch, and began to strip it.

Trouble is, you stand up to the Pentagon generals, you're in deep shit. Just like . . .

Dan started to get up, but his boots slipped and he almost slid over the edge of the rock. He sat, breathing hard, and for just a second he felt dizzy and nauseated.

What had happened today was no different from what had happened ten million times before. Dad said the only things that mattered were the standards you set for yourself. Bull. When did he ever get to set his own standards, decide anything for himself? Even with something as minor as going to summer school!

Hell, he wanted some time off, away from studying, before he hit the university in the fall. You'd think Dad could see that. Fat chance. Roald Ulvang saw things one way—his. And he was always there in the background, saying, "Do it this way, do it my way, forget your way."

Always.

Back when school was so easy there wasn't anything to talk about, it had been Scouts. Dad had him tracked for an Eagle Scout from the day he joined up, decided which badges he'd get, how he was going to get them, which camp he'd go to. Oh, yeah, camp. One summer he'd wanted to go back to the camp he'd gone to the summer before, because he'd had so much fun and knew the same guys would be there. But no way. Dad decided he needed more water experience, so he had to go to the new camp, the one with the lake.

The one where he'd do the mile swim.

That about killed him.

Only thing that saved him was Will, sitting there on that raft, calling out the laps, telling Dan to keep going when all he wanted to do was just sink quietly under that cold blue water so he wouldn't have to swim it again. But he kept going, getting madder with every lap, furious with himself that it wasn't easier for him to do this.

Dan shifted on the rock. That was the first time they really got to know each other. Will didn't have any trouble with the mile swim, or putting up the tent or learning the knots or steering the canoe. But the best part was he didn't say anything when Dan had trouble, when the tent collapsed three times before Dan got the knots right and when Dan dropped the paddle in the deepest part of the lake.

Will would just smile and shrug.

Dan wished Will were here right now.

The sun was gone. Below him on the slope, the dogs ran in a halo of gold, the last of the sunset setting the edges of their fur on fire. Far below, where the foothills leveled out, he saw one light, the one from Sarah's room.

"Why can't you stand up to him, Ulvang?" he whispered. "Or don't you have guts enough?"

He pulled his legs up, elbows clamped to his sides. He had never felt so alone. Sitting in the open doorway of an airplane was a snap compared to this.

But he'd sat in that doorway, knew how it felt to fall into space. He'd learned to control the fall. For a minute he lived it again, air in his face, world open on all sides— top, bottom, left, right. Nothing holding him up or down or back. Nothing pushing him—just alone and free. So different from how he felt this afternoon with his dad staring at him across that patch of dirt, staring him into saying yes one more time.

"Hey, I'd face the Pentagon any old day," he muttered, slapping his boot with the paper. "Any time."

Getting late. Dad would be wondering where he was, wanting his help with the tomatoes. Dan put his head down on his knees and closed his eyes, shutting out the reddened sky, the dogs, the sagebrush lining the trail that stretched toward home.

He was back swimming those laps, only the water was dark and he wasn't sure he'd make it this time.

CHAPTER NINE

Night on the Porch

For the third time, Sarah erased the lettering on the poster board and started over. She couldn't seem to get the letters straight, not sloppy and lopsided. But she wanted a decent-looking poster to replace that streaky monstrosity Kris kept toting around, no matter how long it took.

And it was taking forever. She sat back on her heels and pushed her hair out of her eyes. She had to work on the paper tonight, too. She looked at her desk, at the books and papers flopping there in mass disorder.

"Forget it. Concentrate," she thought, and she bent over the poster again, trying big fat letters this time, looping and curving around each other. END THE WAR IN . . .

She heard a car door slam. Dan was home. She hurried

81

a little on VIETNAM, trying to finish one line she could keep before Mom called her to dinner.

"Sarah!"

"Oh, rats!" She was on the N. "Coming," she called. "In a minute," she said into the poster board.

"Sarah." Mom stood at the door.

"I just want to finish this, Mom."

"Honey, Will's here."

Sarah looked up at her mother, brushing at the hair that tickled her nose.

"He wants to talk to you on the porch. He wouldn't come in." Mom made a funny, grinning face. "You two cooking up something?"

Sarah frowned at her mother, then shrugged. "He probably wants me to look at his paper." She stood up and looked down at the poster, pulling her sweater straight. "This is such a mess. Doesn't look right at all."

She padded down the hall to the front door, wondering why he wouldn't come in, hoping she didn't look too awful. Funny how the thought of Will waiting out on the porch made her feel as if all the parts of her body were disconnected and she had to pay close attention to make everything work right.

He was standing at the very edge, hands in his back pockets, looking down the drive to the highway. Sarah reached for the porch light, but changed her mind and pushed open the door.

"Hi, Will." She stepped onto the porch.

"Hi." He turned. "You busy?"

Sarah shook her head. "No, I wasn't doing much." She walked to the edge of the porch to stand beside him. "Dan's not here. He's out at the airfield."

Will nodded. "Yeah, he told me yesterday he was jumping today. Tried to talk me into going again."

"He would." Sarah laughed, pulling her sweater closed around her. She was shivering suddenly. "Don't let him talk you into it."

"Don't worry. No way I'm going ten thousand feet up in the air."

Sarah shivered again. She didn't want Will to know she was cold, didn't want to force him to go inside or make him hurry away. She clenched her teeth to keep them from chattering.

"I came out because I want to talk to you."

"Oh, the paper. How's Audie Murphy?"

He swatted at the porch railing with one hand. "I'm still reading that one book. It's pretty good." He shrugged. "I'll get it done. No sweat." He leaned against the railing, then straightened, shoving his hands back into his pockets. "I wanted to ask if you'd go to the prom with me. Unless you're going with somebody else?"

Sarah looked at him, almost expecting to see him duck his head or look away. But he was looking right at her, waiting.

"No. I mean, I'm not going with anyone else. Let me ask Mom, see if it's OK." She reached for the door, then paused, laughing. "I'm an idiot. I don't have to ask Mom. I'd love to go with you."

"Great." He let out a gust of air. "Wooh, that's really great."

"Wait a minute. Isn't that your birthday?"

"The next day. May twenty-ninth.

"I remember. You've always had a party right before school got out."

"Yeah, this'll be a nice way to celebrate." He looked at his watch. "Look. I gotta get to work." He started down the steps. "See you Monday."

"You have to go? You want to come in a minute? Mom's making spaghetti. Mom and Dad'd love to see you."

"I really can't. I have to be at work in fifteen minutes." But he climbed the steps back toward her. "Saturday night's always busy. Especially after the movies get out." He took his keys out and tossed them from hand to hand, the metal glittering in the light from the open front door behind them. When he missed and the keys clattered to the ground, he bent to pick them up, muttering about being a spas.

Sarah shrugged her shoulders against the cold, wishing she knew how to make them both feel comfortable, easy with each other like before. She almost asked him about the paper again, just for something to say, but knew that wouldn't work. Through the door, mixed with the warm tomato-sweet air, came the sounds of Dad's news show, voices and planes and explosions.

"What's your dad watching? Sounds like fun."

"Oh, some documentary about the war." She stepped

84

to the edge of the porch, coming to stand so close to Will she could bend her elbow and touch him as she leaned out into the darkness.

"Well . . ." He reached out and put one finger on her arm. "I gotta get going. Peach Palace calls." He spun the keys on his finger.

"Thanks for asking me, Will. I'll . . . that'll be really fun."

"I hope so." He stepped back and in the dimness she could barely see his grin. "Be kind of funny, don't you think? You and me? On a date?"

She wasn't sure for a minute, but then she began to laugh, feeling the nervousness slip away. She nodded. "Right. Funny . . . but nice."

"Yeah, I think so, too." He tossed the keys once before backing down the steps. " 'Bye, Sarah." He lifted his hand. "See you Monday."

She watched as he climbed into the truck and backed out carefully around Mom's car and down the drive. She waved once, then shivered again, letting her whole body dance. Standing on tiptoe, she watched Will's lights until they disappeared around the curve in the road. Suddenly she whirled, arms wide, her sweater making wings at her sides, down the steps and out onto the gravel driveway. And she whooped, loud enough to sound over the rumble of the car as Dan pulled up the driveway.

She stepped out of the beam of his lights. She didn't want to talk to anyone for a minute, just wanted to be alone for a little longer. Wanted to have the secret to herself a little longer before everyone else started pushing and pulling at it.

The back door slammed and soon she saw Dan at the kitchen window, looking out, talking around bites of bread. He was always starving after a jump, even when he stopped in town afterward for a hamburger.

She turned back to the dark yard, walking out along the path of rocks leading to Dad's garden. Will. Wow. She giggled. Wow Will.

She heard the screen door slam shut. "Sarah? Dinner."

She turned back and saw Dan standing on the top step.

"Hurry up, I'm starved. Didn't eat all day." He held a heel of bread in his hand, chewing on it as he spoke.

"Why not?"

"Didn't want to stop. Sar, I jumped five times. One right after another. I'm up to nine now, almost up with some of the guys who've been jumping a lot longer. They're letting me work it off out there doing stuff around the hangars between jumps." He bit off a hunk of bread, chewed and swallowed, nodding and smiling, all at once. "God, it was so great. I jumped better than ever, felt so tight and in control, just sailing through that air, coming in so clean and right on the dime." He sailed the bread crust through the dark air and dropped it into his palm. "Bingo!"

Sarah laughed, leaning against the porch rail. "You're crazy. Will's right."

"Oh, yeah, speaking of William, what'd he want?"

She stood straight. "How do you know he was here?"

"Mom told me. So what'd he want?"

"Just to talk." She started toward the door.

"About what?" He leaned one hand against the screen door so she couldn't open it.

She laughed, pushing at his arm. "Why should I tell you? Maybe it was a private conversation."

"Private conversation with you? Will's *my* friend."

"Yeah, well, don't take it too hard. He had something to talk to me about. Something *private*." Pulling his arm down, she opened the door and went in.

Dan went on about jumping all through dinner. They all listened, twirling the spaghetti on their forks, watching his hands swoop and dive as he described falls and landings. Sarah could tell Dad was enjoying it by the questions he asked, by the amused look on his face as he watched Dan. Mom didn't look so entranced by the whole thing and finally she folded her napkin and put her hand on Dan's arm.

"Dan, may I interrupt?"

He looked at her, a bit startled, then filled his mouth with spaghetti, nodding.

"I just wanted to ask Sarah about Will. About why he came over."

Sarah looked quickly at Dan, who was watching her while he chewed. "He just wanted to ask me to the prom." She said it quickly, all in a rush, while she could.

Mom clapped her hands. Dad sat back. "Well, that's fine," he said, smiling at her.

"I knew it was more than the term paper. He looked

too . . . nervous for that," said Mom. "You said yes, didn't you?"

Sarah nodded, grinning.

"Oh, that's wonderful." Mom folded her napkin, smiling at Sarah over the edge. "I'm so glad your first formal dance will be with Will."

"Couldn't ask for better," Dad said.

"I don't believe it." Dan wiped his mouth. "He said he was asking someone. I never thought it would be you."

Sarah made a face as she got up to clear the table.

"Did he happen to mention the paper to you?" Dan said. "Is he working on it?"

"Is that your business? Will can write his paper by himself."

"If he does, it'll be a first." He got up and went into the living room.

"You're so damn cocky!" Sarah muttered. "I don't know how he puts up with you!" She yelled through the door to the living room. "Remember it's your turn to wash."

He came back in and sat at the table. "Tell me when you're through clearing. And hurry. I don't have all night." He flipped open a magazine.

Once her parents took their coffee into the living room, Sarah cleared the rest of the dishes and started to wipe off the table. As she did, she glanced at what Dan was reading. A pageful of faces. Like a yearbook. But all guys.

"What is that?"

Dan turned the magazine to the cover. *Life*. Familiar

white lettering on a block of red against a gray back-ground.

And a face. Blurred, just eyes, nose, and mouth, and a sweep of hair across the forehead. Above the face the words "Faces of the American Dead in Vietnam: One Week's Toll."

Dan opened the magazine again and flipped toward the front. "Twelve pages. Twenty pictures on each page."

"Wow," she murmured. "So many."

"It says these are the pictures and names of two and hundred and forty-two men who died in one week in Vietnam. No special week. An average."

Dan pointed to the last paragraph. "Read this part."

Sarah followed his finger, and read: " 'In a time when the number of Americans killed in this war—36,000—though far less than the Vietnamese losses, have exceeded the dead in the Korean War, we must pause to look into the faces. More than we must know *how many*, we must know *who*.' "

Sarah wrapped her dishcloth around her hand. "What if you opened this and found someone you knew?"

"Yeah, well, a lot of people are having that pleasure right this minute." He stood up and pushed in his chair.

"What pleasure?" Dad came in and put his cup on the counter.

Dan closed the magazine, but his father pulled it toward him. "What's so interesting?" He looked at the cover. "Oh, yes. Quite an issue."

"It's awful. Just look at how many there are." Sarah

turned the pages. Face after face, most in uniform, some in caps and gowns, a few casual shots like you'd find in a scrapbook.

"I can't believe it. This is so sad." Sarah turned the pages, looking at the faces.

"Well, at least they're getting some recognition. That should be a consolation to their families."

"Yeah, Dad, but what about the ones who die next week? And the next? They won't be in *Life* magazine. And what about all the Vietnamese who die every week?"

"Sarah, it's more complicated than that. You wouldn't understand."

He turned to leave.

"Try me. What about the Vietnamese? Or don't they count?"

Her father reached over and closed the magazine in front of her. "Let's not make an issue out of this. These are Americans—we have a right to be proud of them. It's that simple." He straightened and started for the door.

"I'm not proud that they're dead."

He stopped, turned back. "Well, you should be. Proud that someone was willing to make a sacrifice for his country." He leaned over the table toward her, but looking up at Dan. "We're getting more and more cases before the draft board of people who are trying to find any excuse under the sun not to serve. Flimsy excuses about medical problems and personal problems. Makes you wonder about the American youth." He tapped the magazine. "That's why this makes me proud."

He reached up to the shelf for his pipe and tobacco pouch. "Just last week, we had a case from Washington Terrace who mailed in his draft card, saying he was refusing induction."

Sarah watched him work at the pipe, hoping he'd go on. When he didn't, she asked, "What's so bad about that?"

He looked up at her. "You don't know?"

When she shook her head, he said. "Give me your card, Dan."

"What card?"

"Your draft card. Let's see it."

Leaning to one side, Dan pulled out his wallet, flipped it open, and slid a white card out from behind his driver's license. He tossed it on the table in front of him.

"Read the back."

Dan turned the card over, cleared his throat, and read. "Any person who alters, forges, or in any manner changes this certificate may be fined not to exceed ten thousand dollars or imprisoned for not more than five years or both."

"Well, he didn't do anything to his card," Sarah said, but her father shook his head and nodded toward Dan.

"There's more."

Dan sighed and held the card up straight in front of him as he read on. "The law requires you to have this certificate in your personal possession at all times and to notify your local board if . . . " He looked up. "The rest is just about what to do if you get married or move or something."

"I still don't see what that guy did that's so terrible." Sarah frowned at her father.

He reached across the table and took the card from Dan. "This card stands for the draft and a young man's status with regard to the draft. You heard what it says. He has to carry it at all times. The case in question mailed it in, saying he was refusing to go along with the draft. He might as well have burned it. That is an act punishable by law." He leaned back. "It's very clear."

"So what happens to him?"

"We're giving him another chance, bringing his case up again. And if he still refuses to go, we'll turn him over to the authorities." He looked at Dan. "Don't worry, we're giving him all his rights—he has a lawyer, we've told him about his right to appeal, all of that."

"What if he loses the appeal?" asked Sarah.

He nodded toward the card. "As it says, he can go to jail for up to five years. Or pay a fine of ten thousand dollars." He lit the pipe, shaking his head. "Whole thing leaves a bad taste in my mouth."

"Yeah, just imagine what it does to him." Dan turned away from the table and started to fill the sink with dishes.

Their father leaned back, arms crossed in front of him, as Sarah turned the pages of the magazine, studying the faces. They all looked familiar, like guys she might have sat near in class.

"Dad, don't you ever worry about the guys you draft?" she asked. "Even the ones who don't want to go?"

"Sure we do. We're human. But we know it's a necessary evil. And we know what the alternatives are."

"What *are* the alternatives?"

Sarah looked over her shoulder at Dan. He never used that tone of voice with Dad.

"Communism. You know as well as I do that we're fighting in Vietnam to protect our way of life against the Communists. Our freedom. Your freedom to go to school. Your freedom to protest, Sarah. We must support democracy in Vietnam."

"There's no democracy over there." Dan turned off the water. "We didn't allow South Vietnam to hold free elections in 1956. That's when they lost democracy. We interfered then. And we're interfering now."

"Oh. So you know more than the President, the Pentagon, the—"

"Yes, I do. I've studied this and I think—"

"You think you know more than the President? That kind of arrogance is so typical of this movement against our government and so dangerous."

"It's not dangerous to think, to try to find out the truth."

"Let me tell you truth." Dad leaned forward, pointing his pipe at Dan. "Wherever you have Communists, de-

93

mocracy is in danger. Look at Hungary and Poland in 1955, at Czechoslovakia just last year. Now Vietnam."

"The Viet Cong aren't Communists. That's a myth."

"Myth!" Dad sat back in his chair. "Where did you get that? Ho Chi Minh is an ally of the Red Chinese and you know it."

"That's what Nixon wants us to believe, so we'll all shut up and support the war."

"You're saying the President is lying?"

"Yes. If you call propaganda lying. That's all this is—propaganda so we'll all back the war."

"Oh, I see." Their father lowered his voice and looked through the pipe smoke at Dan. "So I guess it wasn't the Red Chinese I fought against in Korea? Is that what you're learning in school? Tell that to the men in my unit who froze to death at the Chosin Reservoir. Tell them they weren't fighting for democracy."

"I didn't say that. I said—"

"There was no democracy in Vietnam is what you said. What will there be if the Communists win? What happens now when the Viet Cong take over a village? They don't set up a polling booth. They take anyone who has opposed them out into the rice paddies and shoot them. Very democratic. Look at Ho Chi Minh's record in North Vietnam. That will tell you what he'll do in the South." Another puff of smoke.

Dan leaned against the counter, running his finger along the edge of the shelf.

"I see people like you up at the college every day," Dad

said, "so sure they're right about things, so sure they know more than anyone in Washington." He leaned forward, through the smoke, staring at Dan. "That kind of talk is dangerous. The government, President Nixon, the Congress, the military, they need the unconditional support of the American people if we are going to win this war. We can't have people questioning the government, running around second-guessing every decision."

Dan started to speak, but his father went on.

"Those people back in Washington know more than we do about the situation over there. Far more. And if all this information tells them we need to support this war, we need to do it. And that's it." His hand swept the top of the table. "And these boys saying they can't support this war, saying they have a religious opposition to fighting . . ." He shook his head. "They're being used to weaken our war effort. I don't blame *them*."

"You mean they're not thinking for themselves," said Dan.

"I wonder sometimes." His father nodded. Sarah looked at them, staring at each other, so much alike. "Difficult as it may be," Dad went on, "we need to follow authority sometimes, Dan. Young people have to obey those who know more than they do, even when it's unpleasant for them."

"Just shut up and follow orders." Dan's voice was quiet.

A long pause while Dad puffed on his pipe, not looking at Dan. Finally he said, just as quietly, "Exactly."

"And don't ask any questions."

95

His father raised his eyebrows, but he didn't answer, just stared at Dan.

Sarah closed the magazine. No one spoke. After a minute Dad picked up the paper and began to read, and when he did, Dan got up and went outside. Sarah waited for him to come back. When he didn't, she finished doing the dishes. As she worked, she watched her father. He didn't say anything, didn't even look at her, just read and smoked in silence. Finally, she draped the wet dishcloth over the sink and left without speaking to him.

Her mother was in the living room, reading. She glanced up and smiled as Sarah went through the room. Sarah knew Mom must have heard every word.

In the door of her room, she stood looking down at her poster. It seemed just as pathetic now as the one Kris had made. How could any of it make any difference, when people felt the way Dad did?

It was all so depressing. The whole evening had been ruined by a pointless argument that didn't solve anything. Those faces in *Life* and her father's tirade had even ruined her happiness about Will and the prom. Damn this war.

She heard Dan come down the hall a few minutes later and wondered if he and Dad had said any more. She stood without moving until she heard a tap on the door and Mom's voice. "Dan?" She wasn't trying to listen, but Mom's voice carried through the window. Mom was telling Dan to understand Dad, to know he really loved him, to remember he'd served in Korea and lost friends there. The kind of things she had come to their rooms for years to tell them. Especially to Dan's room. And tonight, as usual, Dan didn't say much back, just a few grunts and soft answers.

Sarah knew her mother would come to her room next, saying a lot of the same things, using the same tone of voice. As Sarah stuffed the markers back in their case, she wished that once, just once, it would be Dad that was knocking on the door, trying to make them understand.

CHAPTER TEN

King of the Hill

Today's lunch was his favorite: hot dogs, Tater Tots, milk, and pudding. Could have been worse. Could have been mystery meat and lumpy potatoes. Not too many more days to eat this stuff anyway. He hadn't been counting lately. Too much else on his mind.

He hadn't seen Dan since last Friday. They'd been assigned different buildings to clean on the weekend, and what with work and all he just hadn't had time. And he'd planned it so he wouldn't see him the night he'd asked Sarah to the prom. The way her face had looked when he'd asked her—that made it all worthwhile. Now he just had to be sure he had the cash to do it right.

He swung into the cafeteria, looking for a place to sit. Pretty full. Not many people eating out today. Too many tests and too much rain.

He found a seat by Joe Vasquez, who was smiling and talking a mile a minute to a girl behind him, not eating a thing. He swiveled on his stool as Will sat down.

"I got it. I got it! My preenlistment assignment came."

"Great. What'd they give you?"

"My first choice. First Cav. Man, I'm on my way. Watch out, Vietnam!"

"Doesn't surprise me a bit. Congratulations!" He'd seen Joe Vasquez in his ROTC uniform every Wednesday since tenth grade. And Joe was Honor Guard and high point man on the rifle team.

"Hey, Will. How's things?"

Will looked up. Dan stood there, not making any move to sit, so Will moved his tray over an inch or two and Dan straddled the stool and sat down, opened his milk carton, and took a long drink.

"Joe's just telling me about his assignment," said Will.

Dan bit into a hot dog. "Which one?"

"I just talked to my recruiter and he told me I could get assigned to the First Cavalry. I'll be at Fort Ord two weeks after graduation. Basic training and then on to the best fighting unit in the United States Army."

Dan stared at him. "And you're *happy* about that?"

Will glanced at Dan, frowning. He turned back to Joe. "Go on." He pushed his tray back, watching Joe's face while he talked. He had never seen Joe this excited.

"Will they send you to Vietnam?" Dan asked.

"If they don't, I'll request a tour there."

"Why?"

Joe wadded up his napkin. "That's where the action is right now. You want to get ahead in the military, you go to 'Nam. That's the way it is."

"Yeah, but—"

"And we're fighting for our way of life over there. That's important."

"You sound like my father."

Will shot Dan a glance. His tone of voice sounded ugly.

Joe shrugged.

"Have you read anything about what's going on in Vietnam?" Dan stuck his fork in another hot dog, then put it down. "Do you know anything about the politics of the war?"

Oh, god, thought Will, here we go.

"A little." Joe smiled. "But something tells me you know a lot more."

"To start with, Americans are not exactly loved in Southeast Asia, whatever your recruiter told you. We've been messing up their country since World War Two, fixing elections, buying off officials, even"—Dan paused and looked at both of them—"murdering people who got in our way. Every president since Truman has been messed up in it. We've done everything we could to destroy democracy in Vietnam. Is that what you mean by the American way of life?"

Tapping his fork against the tray, Dan smiled at Joe. Looking like king of the hill. So damn sure of himself.

"That's a load of garbage," Will said.

"Prove it,"

"I can't. I haven't studied it like you have. But I don't believe the President is out to ruin democracy anywhere. Besides, how do *you* know? Did you call up Nixon and ask him?" Will shook his head. "You been talking to Kris, reading her papers? You believe that stuff?"

"Well, Sarah does. You talk to her about it?"

Will looked at his tray. No, he and Sarah didn't talk about the war. He knew how she felt. She'd made it very clear that day in the student union. He was glad she wasn't around to hear Joe's news. It was bad enough to be caught between Dan and Joe. Damn, this war was a mess when you really had to think about it.

Dan was going on. "I've been doing some reading on my own." Sure he had. Dan had read at least one book on every subject. And he'd turn this into an argument, like always. One he had to win.

Will slammed his silverware down on the tray. "What's the point of talking about it all the time? It's on the news every night, it's in the papers. You can't get away from it."

"What's the point of talking about it? Are you serious, man? You noticed who's fighting in the rice paddies these days?"

"Well, you won't be," said Joe. "So why do you care? Isn't this just another intellectual exercise for you, Dan?"

Dan stared at him. "Hey, I carry a draft card just like you do. I've got a lot of stake in this, too."

"Yeah, but you also got all those college scholarships

in your pocket, so it's not quite the same for you as it is for me or Will. Look, Dan, nothing against you, because you'd go to college even without the war going on. But a lot of guys are getting college deferments, sitting around for four easy years, and screaming their heads off about how bad the war is. Calling GIs babykillers, sucking up to the enemy—all without risking their own tails." Joe leaned forward, facing Dan over the trays. "That really burns me."

Dan didn't look down. "I still say the war is wrong. And I don't know if GIs are killing babies or not, but some bad stuff is happening over there. And you know it."

Joe leaned back. "That's why good men need to go. So the bad stuff is stopped." He stood up. "And man, that's where this GI is going." He picked up his tray and left.

Will sat watching Joe weave through the crowd, then turned to Dan. "See?"

"See what?" Dan tipped the milk carton back.

"The way he is." Will looked at Joe, dumping out his tray into the garbage can. "He's got it all together. He knows what he's doing with his life."

"So what? Doesn't everybody?"

Will looked back at Dan. "I don't."

"What are you talking about? You do, too. You know what you're doing, where you're headed."

"I used to think I did. But when I see someone like Joe, I know I'm kidding myself."

"That's just the end-of-the-year jitters. We've all got them. Look, we're almost through, you're passing everything, you got—"

Will shook his head. "It isn't enough. I'm coasting. I'm barely passing. In all my classes."

"Next year will be different. We can really concentrate on stuff without worrying about SAT scores or all the other Mickey Mouse stuff we put up with now." Dan leaned back. "You watch. It'll be better at the university."

"Dan, this isn't the Twilight Zone here. We both know I'm not going to be at the university. I won't even be at the college. Unless I'm there sweeping up." Will looked around a minute, at the talk and laughter and clatter of the cafeteria. "You know, teachers sort of look through me. As if I'm not really there. They're not like that with you. They light up when you talk. And that won't change. No way."

"What are you talking about?"

"It's time you faced the fact I'm not going to the university next year. Or to any school. It'd be a waste of my time."

"Will . . ."

Will shook his head. "I'm not shitting you, man."

"We've always talked about going to college."

"*You've* talked about it. I've listened. Like everything."

"That's crap."

"No, that's the truth. Look at me." Will put his hands on his chest. "Think about it. You know me. I'm not cut out for college, even if I could make it."

"That's stupid." Dan shoved his tray to one side. "If you don't go to college, what'll you do?"

Will shrugged. "I don't know. Get a job."

"You'll be drafted."

"Maybe. That's not the end of the world."

"Not the end of the world? Will you *listen* to yourself?"

"Right, Dan, it's stupid and you're the only one around here with any brains, the only one who knows anything." Will leaned back, feeling his face grow hot. "Yeah, I'm too stupid to know what I'm doing, me and Joe both. Maybe we should have come to you first so you could tell us what to think, huh?"

Dan didn't speak, just stared across the table at Will. So cool. So in control.

"Tell me how to run my life, Dan, fix me up with girls, write my papers so I can pass."

Dan looked away.

"It's just like with Joe. You think you know everything about everything. Even if you haven't got any idea. Don't you think that maybe Joe knows more about what the army is doing in Vietnam than you do? But you think because you've read a book on the subject that you know the truth."

"This is so ridiculous. What is—"

"You know, I'm not the only one who's sick and tired of your attitude, this idea you have that you know everything. I wanted to talk to Joe and you had to come along and turn the whole thing into a lecture on how messed up everyone else is. Everyone but Daniel Ulvang."

Vietnam to make sure bad stuff didn't happen. Who was Joe kidding?

"So what do you think?" Sarah said over his shoulder. He glanced at the rearview mirror.

"About what?"

"These." She waggled her head, making the long earrings she wore bounce and tangle in her hair.

"I don't know. Why?"

"Kris loaned them to me. Do you think they're too much for the prom?"

"Geez, Sar, I don't know. Ask Mom."

"Oh, you know Mom's taste. I love these." Sarah ran her fingers down the filigree and over the beads. She looked at Dan in the mirror, her nose wrinkling. "Do you think Will would like them?"

"Hell, Sarah, why don't I turn around and we can go back and ask him?" He hit the steering wheel with his hand. "It doesn't matter what he likes. Wear what you like."

"OK, OK. Sorry I asked." Sarah sat back in the seat, rolling down her window. "Forgive me for living."

"I'll try." He glanced in the mirror. "Hey, Sar, is Will doing that paper for Quinn?"

"I don't know. Why don't you turn around and we can go back and ask him?"

After he turned up the drive, Dan turned off the car and leaned for a minute on the steering wheel. "Give me a break, OK? Today has been the shits. Just tell me if he's doing the paper."

Sarah got out and looked in the window at him. "I know he started it. But I don't know how far along he is."

Dan nodded and got out of the car, balancing his books under one arm. Quinn had checked outlines and note-cards for the paper today and Dan had thought for sure that Will would panic. But when Quinn called Will's name he'd stood up, picked a notebook off his desk, and walked to the front of the room. Quinn had looked at the notebook, seemed to be asking Will questions. And Will had answered them, not just standing there looking miserable, the way he usually did.

Will hadn't asked Dan for help. So if he was doing the paper, he was on his own. That would be a first.

Snack and chores and a stab at the mountain of home-work and it was time for the news. Dan opened his door so he could hear, but he didn't go into the living room. He hadn't watched the news with his father since the blowup the other night. Dad wouldn't say anything, but he'd look at Dan with those stone-cold eyes and the whole argument would lie there under the surface just waiting for someone to cough wrong.

Funny, Dan was thinking more about the war than he ever had before. Since that night, he had vowed to learn everything he could about this mess. Quinn had given him some books and told him to read *The New York Times* if he really wanted to know what was going on. He said that Walter Cronkite's nightly body count on the news wasn't the whole story.

So what was the whole story? Dan looked at the books stacked beside his bed, the ones he read every night once he'd packed in the homework. *Guide to the Draft* and *We Won't Go*, both Quinn's books. And all the pamphlets from the ACLU and the Quakers. *Street Without Joy* was really keeping him up at night. This war was more of a mess than he'd thought. Sarah was right. Those pictures in *Life* magazine weren't the half of it. None of those faces were Vietnamese. And it was the Vietnamese who were getting the shaft in this war. Literally.

Joe, all convinced he'd make a difference. He was just going to get his head blown off.

Dan rubbed his face. But he wasn't ready to lay all this on Dad yet. He needed more time to put the mess of figures and dates and atrocities together into a watertight argument. He never again wanted to be pounded into the ground by Dad and his frozen buddies at the Chosin Reservoir.

Good old Sar was hanging in there, though. She'd started sitting in the chair he usually sat in and was there every night taking notes on the news. The first time, when Dad asked her what she was doing, she'd said she wanted more background. Dan could still hear her. "I'm helping out up at the student union all next week and I want to know what's going on over there." She'd tipped her head a bit and studied the book in her lap, glancing up at Dad over the top.

Way to go, Sar.

But tonight, as usual, it wasn't long before Dan heard

their voices, Sarah's rising like it always did when she got mad, Dad's steady drone on and on underneath.

"You know better, Sar. It won't work," Dan muttered.

He tapped the desk in front of him with his pencil before closing his book. He just couldn't concentrate. Everything got in the way.

Weird how everybody got pissed when they talked about the war. Usually you watched the news and it just was so much noise. And here were Sarah and Dad in there yelling at each other. He heard Sarah say, very loudly, "Everyone has a personal responsibility to—" Dad interrupted her, but she repeated it. "Everyone has a personal responsibility."

Maybe Will talked about the war the way he did to get him ripped, especially if he felt he was being shoved around. Like the other night between him and Dad. Sure, they were arguing about the war. But he knew the hot anger he felt was because he was still so ripped at Dad about summer school and his AP scores. That's the only reason he'd dared stand up to Dad at all.

That and Dad's smugness about obeying orders. Easy for him to say. No one was telling him to go lay down his life for his country.

Maybe Will was playing the same game he had the other night.

Maybe all this talk about not going to college and feeling like he was drifting and about the war was just a game. An end-of-the-year senioritis game that would blow over once the year was over. When Will could shut the books and forget it all for the summer.

Shoving aside his chemistry book, Dan put his head down on the desk and shut his eyes. In the air, up there sitting in the open door of that plane, all space waiting for him, no one yelling in his ear . . . that was heaven.

He thought how wild it would be to jump with Will, both of them up there, spinning around like two big eagles. That would be a gas.

CHAPTER TWELVE

Night at the Prom

"Sarah?" Mom's voice. "Can I come in?"

"Sure." Door was already opening.

"How you doing, honey? Need any help?"

"Oh, yes, Mom." Sarah turned, hands at the straps of her slip, teetering a little in her high heels. "Could you mend the hem on my dress? It pulled out when I was trying it on."

Her mother turned up the hem. "It sure did. I'll fix it." She disappeared into the hall.

Sarah brushed her hair out arm's length, watched as it fell back onto her shoulders. She shivered. "I hate this," she muttered. "I wish we were going to a movie and I could wear my old jeans and sweatshirt and not worry about my hair. I feel so . . . silly."

She turned and unpinned a photograph from her bulletin board, Will standing beside her on Malan's Peak. She touched his face, then pinned it back, next to the pictures she'd taken of the dogs.

"Your father"—Mom's voice coming down the hall again—"takes my sewing basket and leaves it on the workbench." She settled herself in the chair, the dress draped over her skirt. "This will take just a minute."

Sarah sat on the bed, watching her mother. It was Mom who was excited about this, about Sarah's first formal dance, first flowers, all that. Mom was so . . . what? romantic, maybe.

Sarah watched her mother smooth the hem on her lap and pull out a length of thread. "It's hard for me to believe you three are old enough for all this, the boys graduating, you and Will out on a date." She put up her hand and looked at Sarah. "I know you're tired of hearing it, but I hate to see you grow up so fast."

"I know."

"No, you don't. Not until you have your own." She sighed. "I hope Dan has fun with . . . what's her name?"

"Linda Collins."

"Is she a nice girl?" Mom bit off the thread and shook the dress out.

Sarah shrugged. "I guess. I don't really know her."

"You know, I worry about Dan sometimes. He never dates the same girl twice, and when you think about it, Will is one of the few friends he has."

Sarah pulled at the bedspread. "The only one," she muttered.

"What?"

Sarah sat up and took the dress from her mother. "Thanks, Mom." She slipped it over the hanger. "It's a wonder Will is his friend. Dan can be so . . . arrogant and stubborn."

"Is he like that at school?"

Sarah nodded.

Her mother tightened her lips. "Just like his father," she said, biting off each word.

Startled by the tone of her mother's voice, Sarah looked at her, but Mom was bent over, fussing with the hem again, and didn't say any more.

After a minute Mom smiled and, reaching up, brushed Sarah's hair with the back of her hand. "You two have a wonderful time. Will is a jewel."

She stood on the front porch, looking down the drive where it curved onto the highway. She glanced down at her dress. In the light from the living room, the purple and rose of its tropical flowers looked dark, almost disappearing into the green background. She sighed, pulled the waist of the dress down, pushed a little at her bra. Her few dates before tonight had been for basketball games, stomps, or movies and Peach Palace. For the hundredth time she wished that was where they were going tonight. I'm just not cut out to wear a long dress, she thought.

Lights on the highway, turning up the drive. The shape of the truck, its rattle. This is it, she thought.

114

Will climbed out of the truck, stopping to rearrange his jacket, fiddle with his tie. Sarah stood on the steps, watching him, until he looked up and saw her.

"Oh, hi. Didn't see you." He reached into the truck and took out a white box and came toward her, holding it out. "Flowers."

"Thanks, Will." She took out the gardenia and stood in the light of the truck to pin it on.

"You look nice."

She grimaced at him. "I just hope I don't fall over in these heels."

"I'll catch you if you do." He opened the truck door for her and stood aside while she gathered her skirts and climbed in. More than ever, she felt weird. She wondered if Will felt the same, and knew he did when he passed in front of the truck and she saw in the lights that he was fiddling with his tie again. She sighed.

"Oh, please don't let me do anything too stupid," she whispered.

They didn't say much on the drive into town, just a little chatter about who was going with whom, what teachers would be there as chaperones, a little laughter about teachers dancing with each other. When they got to the country club, Will parked the truck and they walked into the lighted hallway, smiling at people they hardly recognized in their dressup clothes, then on into the dark dance floor, only one light over the refreshment table.

She didn't see Dan when he first arrived. During a pause between dances, as she and Will stood surrounded

115

by other dancers, trying to cool off, she looked up and saw him standing by the glass doors to the patio, hands in his pockets, Linda's arm through his, looking around the dance floor. Like the king has arrived, she thought. But even she had to admit he looked wonderful, white jacket setting off his wide shoulders and the light from the hall glancing off his hair, longer than anyone else's in the room.

"You want something to drink?" Will asked her.

"Sure. What do they have?"

"Probably punch," He grinned. "Want some?"

"Sure."

At the table, they both drank, the sweet sticky stuff not doing much to quench her thirst.

The music slowed and Will put his arms around her for a slow dance. "White Rabbit." One of her favorites. Even if this group wasn't exactly Jefferson Airplane. She shut her eyes. Will was a good dancer, better than she'd expected. And once she'd taken off her shoes, she could keep up with him.

"Hey, Will."

Dan. Smiling at them, his hand on Will's shoulder.

"Hi, Dan."

"Hey, buddy, happy birthday."

She looked up at her brother. Dan never called anybody "buddy." He hated names like that. She stepped back, but Will kept hold of her hand.

"It's not till tomorrow."

"I know. Eighteen years old. The start of the good times."

Will shrugged. "Yeah, I guess so." He started to turn back to Sarah.

"I've got your present. Come on out on the porch. I want to give it to you."

"Later. We're dancing."

"I want Sarah to see this, too. Come on. Linda's in the bathroom. Just us three." Dan started through the mob, twisting between dancers, not looking back to see if they were following.

Will looked at Sarah. "You mind? Take just a minute."

"It's OK. Let's go." Why was Dan making such a big deal about a present?

Out on the porch, in the cool air, Dan was waiting, his hands behind him on the railing that curved down to the lawn below. He smiled at Will and Sarah. "Good dance, isn't it?"

"Yeah, it's fine." Will shoved his hands in his pockets.

"Look, what you said the other day is really true." Dan shifted against the metal bar. "I was a jerk and I apologize. I don't mean to butt in, I just want to help." He let out a gust of air.

Sarah felt Will's hand tighten around hers. She didn't know what Dan was talking about, but she had an idea. Sounded like Dan had been a royal jerk this time, if it had gotten to Will.

"So, anyway . . ." Dan laughed shortly. "Your present.

117

I'm sorry about the way things have been between us lately and I hope this makes up for it. It's something I really want you to have."

"Great." Will stepped toward him.

Dan reached into his jacket pocket, pulled out an envelope, and held it out. Sarah watched as Will opened the envelope, shook out a piece of paper and read it, then looked up at Dan. They stared at each other until Will shoved the paper back in the envelope.

"Thanks." Neither of them moved.

"What is it?"

Will bit his lip, looking over at her. "Dan's given me a free parachute jump. One free ride. Dated next Monday."

Dan grinned at Sarah. "That's Memorial Day. No school. I told you I'd find a way to get him in the air. And you'll love it. I promise you. It'll blow your mind."

"Good for that day only?"

"Yeah, it's then or never."

"What if I say never?"

Dan hunched his shoulders, shoving his hands deeper into his pockets. "What's the big deal? Sure you'll do it."

"Come on, Sarah, let's dance." Will turned his back on Dan and opened the door to the dance floor.

"So what do you say, Will? You'll jump?"

Will paused a minute, not speaking, letting Sarah go through the door ahead of him. Once in the middle of the dance floor, he turned, grabbed her hand, and pulled her up next to him. She tried to move with him, but she stumbled, caught the hem of her skirt in her bare foot. "Oh, damn." And as she bent to pull the skirt straight, she began to cry. "Damn it, Sarah," she muttered. "Don't *do* this." She rubbed at her cheeks with her wrist.

"Hey, Spencer." Dan pulled at Will's arm. "What's it going to be?"

Sarah peered up at them, pretending to fuss with her skirt until she could control her eyes.

"I want to dance with Sarah. We'll talk about it later."

"No, I want an answer now. You owe me that much."

"OK!" Will shouted. "I'll jump. OK? You happy? Now will you back off?"

Sarah straightened, hands still at her cheeks. She saw people around them stop dancing for a minute, but the music kept on beating, a song about Kansas City, the guitar wandering behind the words. Will grabbed her hand. "Come on. Let's get out of here."

Over her shoulder, Sarah saw Dan watch them and then turn and put his arms around Linda.

Will didn't speak until he'd parked the truck on a level spot just off the canyon road. When Sarah let go of the door handle she realized she'd gripped it so hard it had left marks in the palm of her hand. She smoothed her skirt out and pulled her hair over one shoulder. She looked at Will. He was staring out over the hood of the truck, out over the boulders that littered this stretch of foothill. Sarah looked, too, out over the lights of town spangling the valley. They sat for a moment, silent.

119

Say something, Sarah thought.

"Why don't we—" she began.

"I shouldn't have—" Will said.

They laughed, stopped talking, finally looked at each other for the first time since they'd left the parking lot of the club. Will fiddled with his tie, finally loosened it completely. Sarah watched him, thinking how different he looked tonight. How much older in his white jacket.

She took a deep breath. "Will, I'm sorry about what Dan did."

He turned quickly, holding out one hand, almost, not quite touching her. "Let's not talk about it, OK? It's way too serious for a night like this."

"But I'm so mad about what he did. I want—"

"Sar, please. I don't want to spoil things." He gathered up a lock of her hair and twisted it gently. "OK?"

"But, Will, you haven't . . ." She put her hand up on his. "OK, we won't talk about it. This is too nice."

"You wish we'd stayed at the dance?"

"No, this is more fun." Suddenly Sarah started to laugh. "Will, I just realized I left my purse back at the dance. And my shoes!"

"Huh?" He turned and looked at her, and down at her toes wiggling on the rim of the dashboard. He started to laugh, then stopped. "Oh, geez, I'm sorry. We'll go back."

"No!" She put her hand over the keys. "No. I want to stay here."

"But your shoes . . ."

"I'll get them tomorrow. Or . . . whenever. I want to stay here with you."

He leaned forward and turned on the radio, then lifted her hand off the keys. "You want to dance?"

"Here?"

He tipped his head toward the door. "Plenty of room out there."

"Um, it's a bit rocky though."

"I know." He reached behind him, started tossing heavy things around in the back of the cab. "I think there's a pair of . . ." His voice was muffled. "These!"

"Oh, no!" Sarah gasped, laughing as she reached up for the rubber boots he held out to her. "What great boots."

"Yeah, they even buckle. Here." He grabbed her right foot, slid it into the boot, and buckled it tightly, did the same with the other foot. Sarah lay back against the door, laughing, laughing, until she felt she might start to cry.

"This is crazy."

"Come on, Sar. I wanna dance." He pulled her out after him, put his arms around her, swung them both for a moment to the music, slowed to a closer step. Back at the club she'd wondered where Will had learned to dance so well, how he knew how to hold her so casually. Now she stopped wondering, let the music take over her head, let Will move them through the cool darkness. "A Whiter Shade of Pale" from the radio. She felt his hand on her back, moving slowly up and down, over the fabric of her dress, up to her neck, under her hair, where his hand moved gently for a moment, then down to her waist, to move her around a rock.

The music stopped and the deejay started babbling about "redi-Quik," the latest in fast foods. Sarah felt Will touch her cheek gently, kiss her nose. She opened her eyes. Stars behind his head, all around him. She forgot for a minute where she was.

"Wow." Will let out a long breath. He shook his head and repeated, "Wow."

They stood without moving. When Will took off his jacket and put it around her shoulders, she realized how cold her arms were. From farther down the hill they heard the sound of cars, shouts, another car radio.

"I guess we're not the only ones with this idea."

"I guess not." Sarah's voice wasn't quite steady.

"You want to go back in the truck?" he asked.

"No. Do you?"

He laughed. "Heck, no. This is perfect." He looked at her, reached out to touch her face. "Why did I wait so long?" He took a handful of her hair, lifted it, let it fall through his fingers. "Looks like a waterfall. I've always loved your hair."

She closed her eyes, and suddenly she felt his hands on her shoulders and then on her face and then he kissed her, so lightly she thought he had touched her lips with his fingers. She caught her breath, let her hand tighten on the back of his neck, until she caught her fingers in the curls that covered his collar and she relaxed against him, moving with him into the kiss.

She could think only about the music and Will, his breath on her cheek, his hand on her neck, his whisper in her ear. She ducked her head and took a step back, to catch her breath, to wait, wait a minute. When she looked up, he reached out to her with one hand, the stars still circling his head. "Sarah, I'll miss you."

She pulled his arms around her again and covered his mouth with her hand so he couldn't say any more.

CHAPTER THIRTEEN

Dog-Run Duty

Dan's hands shook as he poured out a cup of coffee. He leaned against the counter, watching the steam. It was hot, too hot, and he could only sip at it. Didn't matter. He wasn't in any hurry. He stared across the kitchen, watching the early-morning light on the opposite wall, listening for sounds of anyone getting up. Mom or Dad. Or Sarah. If she was even home.

The calendar for May showed a stand of aspen, just turning green. He took another sip, staring at the picture a moment. Then he looked back at the cup in his hand. Maybe if he added milk he could drink it. He needed it or he'd fall over before he got to bed.

Below the calendar hung the chore schedule. "Oh, right," he muttered. "My turn for dog-run duty yesterday." He scuffed across the kitchen and bent to check. For a minute his eyes wouldn't focus and he pushed his glasses up on his forehead to rub at his eyes. "Damn, I'm wasted."

He straightened and ran his finger down the sheet until he found May 28, then across to the column marked "Dog run." He grunted. "Yep, my turn."

He pressed the heel of his hand to his forehead, scratching at his scalp. Better do it before I hit the sack, he thought, or Dad'll be on me because I didn't do it yesterday. He yawned, stretching widely, coffee cup tipping in his hand. "Some people live by the book, but here at the Ulvangs' we live by the schedule." He took another slow sip of coffee. "Or die by it," he muttered.

Oh, boy.

What a night.

He grinned as he poured the coffee down the drain and rinsed out the cup, thinking about Linda. They'd had a great time—at the club and afterward. So why was he in such a blue funk?

Closing his eyes, he leaned on the sink. He'd made things worse. He'd been trying to make up for being a shit the other day and he'd just gotten in deeper.

He reached out to the geranium on the windowsill and broke off a browning blossom. All he wanted was for Will to know that feeling when he tipped out of the plane, that lonely, all-bets-are-off, wide-eyes-to-the-sky joy.

Joy.

And that was when he'd blown it, when Will didn't seem to catch the joy part. When he acted like he'd been handed a train ticket to nowhere.

"What if I say never?" he'd said.

What you get for trying.

Behind the house, the mountains were showing color. As Dan neared the dog run, he heard the dogs waking up, Buff's yawn as he stretched, Countess's short, sharp barks. He unwrapped the hose, pulled it into the pen, pushing aside the dogs as they rushed to greet him.

"Get away, you guys." He bumped them roughly as they circled his legs, growling happily. "Hey, be quiet. You'll wake everyone up."

He wondered what time it was. He stopped a minute, hose in his hand. He'd taken Linda home at five, driven around for a while, then home. Must be close to six by now.

"It's early, so be quiet," he told Countess, who pressed against him. "Yeah, I'll even give you a brushing." He ran his hands down the dog's warm golden coat. "Even though it is Sarah's turn."

After he shoved Buff out of the pen, he got out the broom and shovel from behind the doghouse and began to work at the wads of dog hair and dirt in the corners.

He was spreading blankets and rugs from the doghouse over the fence when he saw Sarah coming up the drive. He looked quickly out to the road. No sign of the truck. What'd Will do, dump her on the road and take off? He looked at Sarah again. She wasn't walking. She was tiptoeing, sort of hopping from rock to rock, holding her dress up with one hand. When she got to the grass, she glanced up and saw him. She stopped, dropped her skirt, and pushed her hair away from her face.

Dan stepped out of the dog run. Both dogs ran to Sarah and she bent over them, ruffling their ears. "What are you doing, Sarah? Trying to sneak in?"

Sarah looked up at him, pulling a face, as she lifted one foot. "Gravel's hard to walk on when you're bare-footed."

Dan walked down the slope toward her. "Where are your shoes?"

"Back at the club. Remember, Will and I left in a hurry last night? I forgot them." She started toward the house, then turned back to face her brother. "Why are you doing chores now?"

He shrugged. "Get 'em done."

"When'd you get home?"

"A little while ago. How's Will?"

Sarah sat down in the grass and immediately Buff pushed at her arm with his nose. Sarah pulled the dog's big head onto her lap, smoothing the long ears out over her dress. Dan watched the dog huff out his jowls, all contentment.

"He's fine," Sarah said.

"Have a good time?"

"Yeah. Did you?"

"Did he say anything?"

"Yeah, we talked a lot last night. Well, actually, more

127

like this morning." She laughed a little, bent over Buff's head. He heard her mutter something.

"Well, what'd he say?" He sat down in the grass by her and pushed at her arm.

"About what?" She was blushing and she brushed at her cheeks with both hands.

"Oh, come on. Did he say anything about the jump?"

"No."

Dan took in a quick breath. "Not at all?"

"No. Did you expect him to?"

Dan pulled at the grass, tossing it onto Buff's flank. "Yeah, sort of. He was kind of upset."

"Yes, he was. But he didn't want to talk about it. He said it would ruin the evening."

Ruin the evening? Damn him. Dan jumped to his feet and stalked up the hill to the dog run, grabbed the rugs and blankets off the fence, and threw them into the doghouse. Sarah followed him and stood outside the fence, her fingers in the mesh.

"But do you want to know what I think, brother dear?"

"Not especially."

"I think what you did stinks."

Dan pulled a rug straight. "Don't start, OK?"

"Why not? *You* started this."

"Started what? Just tell me what I started. I seem to be missing something here."

"You *always* miss something, because you don't listen to what people say, because you think you know everything. Will has been telling you, ever since you started

128

bugging him about jumping, that he didn't want to do it. *He* didn't. *Will Spencer didn't want to jump out of a plane.* But that didn't mean anything to you. You had to have your way." She rattled the mesh against the post. "And then you make it a birthday present, for Pete's sake. Something he can't refuse. You gave him no way out."

"That's bull. You just don't understand."

"Oh, god, do you know how sick I am of hearing that?" She grabbed her hair with both hands, her voice rising. "Just like Dad." She glared at him, her mouth rigid. "You say that when you don't want to talk about something, when you don't want to face up to things. Just like Dad did the other night when he didn't want to talk about the war." She whirled into the pen and stood inches from his face. "It's a cop-out. And you know it."

He'd never seen her this mad. Not little-girl mad, but glittering mad, her eyes sparking as she spat words at him.

He gripped the broom, not wanting to back up. "Come on, Sarah, aren't you getting—"

"What? A little carried away maybe?"

"Yeah, exac— Yeah."

"So what? What's wrong with that? Besides, you don't listen unless someone screams in your face." She leaned toward him and he did back up.

"Just like Dad," she went on. "Always so rational. Always *so in charge*." She said the last words through clenched teeth. "And you're just like him."

129

"OK, so I'm a bastard. So what else is new? Where is this getting anybody?"

"Dan, I'm trying to get you to see that you're going to ruin your friendship with Will. Not just the jump, but everything." She began to pace the pen, running her fingers along the mesh behind her. "And because he's your friend, he won't say anything to you, so I am." She stopped and stared at him. He leaned against the doghouse, staring out through the wire.

"Just take it back. Tell him it was a joke, or that you don't have the money or all the planes broke down or something. It doesn't matter. Just please don't make him jump. Please."

"That's ridiculous. People don't make other people do things. How can I *make* him jump if he doesn't want to?"

"We're not talking about people—we're talking about you and Will. About friends." She pulled her fingers out of the mesh, making it clang. "A subject you apparently know nothing about."

Before he could answer, she turned, pushed past the dogs, and ran down the slope to the house. At the door, she stopped and looked at him. "Dan, you better start learning. Or you'll be sorry." Then she went in, the door sighing shut behind her.

"Or you'll be sorry," Dan mimicked. He picked up the broom, stomped its bristles a few times on the cement floor of the dog run, and hurled it into the corner. "Maybe I already am!" he shouted.

CHAPTER FOURTEEN

Birthday Party

Sarah stepped out of her dress and kicked it onto the bed. She stood a minute looking at it, before picking it up and slipping it over the hanger behind the door. She ran her hand down the skirt. She would never forget this dress.

She picked up her hairbrush and, sitting on the bed, pulled her hair around and began to brush it. It felt good and she brushed harder and harder, back from her forehead, off her neck, around her ears. Felt so good. Get the blood moving around the scalp, Mom always said.

Maybe it would help her calm down.

She dropped the brush and listened. Dan was in the kitchen. She leaned forward and shut the door gently. She couldn't talk anymore right now or she'd end up screaming at him and wake everybody up.

She checked the clock by her bed. Six thirty. She lay back on her pillow. She couldn't see Will until four. Nine and a half hours. How could she wait that long?

She rolled over onto her side. Well, she'd just sleep those hours away. Mom and Dad wouldn't expect her to be up. She closed her eyes. Think about the dance, sitting on the hill beside Will, how his curls felt in her fingers, how smooth his skin was in that spot right in front of his ears.

Her eyes opened. She looked out the window at the mountains behind the house. She was too keyed up to sleep. She got out of bed, took the photograph of Will off the bulletin board, and lay down again, holding the picture above her head so she could look at it. It didn't do him justice, mostly because he wasn't smiling. He didn't smile a lot ever, but he had last night, and he'd laughed, probably more than she'd ever heard him laugh before. He'd had a good time, she knew. As much as she had.

She ate breakfast at nine with her parents, took a bath at ten, watched *Gospel Hour* at eleven, wishing Dan could come in so they could laugh about it together, but knowing they wouldn't laugh if he was there, lay down again at twelve, didn't sleep again.

Will's mom was having a party for him—just the family, which meant her and one grandmother. Sarah wondered if Will would put Dan's card on the table with all the others, if he'd even tell his mom, who would probably ask him what Dan had given him. What a present—a parachute jump!

Typical Dan.

He and Will had always given each other presents—GI Joes and baseball cards and, once, a *Playboy* magazine. Sarah knew not because Dan showed anyone, but because she'd found it in his dresser drawer when she was looking for a sweatshirt to borrow—and Will had written something in the front.

She turned over on the bed. *Playboy* magazine, for Pete's sake. She wondered if Will looked at it too, if he thought about those round, silky, golden girls in the pictures a lot. Probably. And he was stuck with her. She grinned. He didn't seem to mind.

Oh, come on, clock, move. She got up and walked to the window, flipped through the books she'd brought home on Friday, not really expecting to get anything done, since all that was left were a couple of tests. No school tomorrow. Memorial Day. That's why Dan had chosen it for the jump—they'd be out of school. Sarah shut the books and looked out the window. She could hear Dad and Mom talking in the garden. Dan? Nowhere in sight.

Yeah, he'd gotten his way. He was probably real pleased with himself.

Maybe Will's grandma would leave early and he would call.

Sarah would just have to wait. He'd said he'd come out at four and she'd see him then. They'd go up the mountain and talk—away from everybody . . . from Dan especially.

By three thirty she was pacing in front of the house. After a while she crunched down the drive a ways to sit on the big rock by the mailbox. All the times Will had come to their house, she had never felt like this. Amazing how one night had turned a perfectly sane, ordered sixteen-year-old girl into a person who couldn't sit still, couldn't seem to catch her breath.

And then he was there, pulling the old truck up in front of her and leaning out the window. "You want a ride?" Grinning in a bright-blue shirt. Honey hair surrounding his face. Brown hand reaching out to her.

They didn't talk much up the mountain. Held hands. Stopped to kiss behind a clump of scrub oak. Tickled each other's cheeks with oat grass. Picnic Rock was too sunny, so they went around behind and found a patch of shade thrown by Castle Rock. Now that he was here, Sarah felt the way she did just before a piano recital—so nervous she could leap to the top of the rock behind her back without losing a breath.

Will told her about his birthday, about the cake and the money his grandmother had given him and the card from his father. Then he told her to turn around a minute.

"What for?"

"Just do it." So she did, and when she turned around again, he was holding out a blue folder.

"Where did that come from?"

"Inside here." He grinned, patting his chest. "Lucky you didn't want me to take my shirt off."

She felt herself grow red, so she looked at the folder again.

"What is it?"

"Look and see."

She opened it slowly, then smiled. "Your paper. Audie Murphy. You did it." She held it out from her, looking at the title page, which read:

Story of a Hero
Audie Murphy

And, half a page down:

William Spencer
American History
Mr. Quinn
May 31, 1969

Will tapped the page. "The best part of this is that for the first time in my life I don't feel it ought to say Daniel Ulvang instead of Will Spencer. I wrote this alone. All by myself." He pointed to himself, making a tough face. "With a little help from a certain really smart and really cute junior, Sarah Ulvang."

She felt herself blush again.

He took the folder, closed it, and set it on a rock. "Don't let me forget that." He put his hands on her shoulder and moved her beside him inside the cool, damp shadow of the rock. She could feel him breathing.

135

"Thanks, Sarah. This means a lot to me. Really." She felt him take a big breath. "Now . . . all I have to get through is that damn jump tomorrow."

She stepped away from him. "Tell Dan no. Say you won't do it."

"You make it sound easy."

"What can he do to you?"

"The jump isn't such a big deal to me, Sar. But it is to Dan. So I jump and I get him off my case. Then I won't have to listen to it anymore." She listened to his breathing. "And, who knows, it might be fun." He circled her back with one arm, put the other hand on the side of her face. "It might not be as bad as I think. I may not be as afraid of heights as I think I am."

"What if you are?"

He shrugged and pulled her closer to him. "Don't think about that. I'm not. I'm just thinking about last night. And right now. And I can only handle thinking about one Ulvang at a time. So Dan will just have to wait."

That afternoon, Sarah remembered wondering what couples were talking about as they stood in the hallways at Wasatch High, ignoring everyone around them, ignoring tardy bells and teachers' calls to get to class. What kept them looking at each other so long, what was the guy whispering to the girl that made her duck her head, smiling and playing with his shirt buttons?

So, Sarah, for the first time you're half of a couple, she thought. Do you know now how easy it is to forget everything else?

And she also remembered the desperation she'd sensed in those couples as they leaned into each other against the hall lockers. She could understand that now, too, and wondered if that was what kept Will from leaving even though he kept saying he had to get home.

Finally they started down the hill, arms around each other, not laughing as much, quiet now that the afternoon was over. Will carried the folder under his free arm, and when they got back to his truck, Sarah took it and leafed through it one more time.

"Does Dan know you've finished this?"

He shook his head.

"You want me to tell him?"

"No. I want to see the look on his face Tuesday when I hand it in. He won't believe it. It'll be fun to surprise him."

"I'll think about you tomorrow."

"Right. Wish me luck."

"I do. I hope you land smoothly."

"I don't worry about landing. It's the flying keeps me up nights."

"Fly right then." And she kept repeating it as he drove away down the highway.

CHAPTER FIFTEEN

The Jump

"All you have to do, Will, is follow directions. When Tom gives you the thumbs-up, get positioned in the doorway of the plane, set your hands and feet, and wait till he pats you on the shoulder. Then you fly!"

"You mean I fall."

"Hey, man, it's no sweat. You'll love it. Trust me."

Dan squeezed Will's shoulder one last time and tugged on the straps that crossed his friend's chest. "Looks like you're all set. Any last words?"

"No." Will couldn't think of anything to say, couldn't make his mind move to think of anything. He knew if he thought very much he'd lose it, completely. Hands hooked in the parachute pack on his chest, he crossed the runway to where the other two jumpers were hoisting themselves into the belly of the plane. Tom, the jump master, stood to one side, watching. Will looked over his shoulder and saw Dan shouldering into his harness and reserve chute. Dan looked up and, grinning, threw Will a wide, high thumbs-up. Will nodded and turned toward the plane.

When the men in front of him had settled on the bench along the side of the plane, he pulled himself up into the open hatch, feeling the strange pull of the straps around his chest and between his legs. He felt hemmed in, wedged into the jumpsuit. As he sat down, he looked out at the hangars, the offices, the cars parked behind the fence. He was glad Sarah wasn't there.

Dan pulled himself up into the plane and nudged Will. "Relax, man. Relax and let your mind go."

The plane's engine stuttered, died, coughed alive, caught, and held. They all lurched a little as the plane started to roll. The other first-time jumpers looked at each other and grinned, then looked out the open door of the plane, watching the ground speed by and drop away as the plane lifted off.

Will leaned his head back against the wall, eyes closed. He felt his hair pressing against his forehead under the helmet.

Relax and let my mind go, he thought. He wondered if Dan could really do that, if it was as easy for him as he made it sound.

Trouble was, only place his mind wanted to go was back down. Far away from that open doorway a foot to his left.

He reached out to steady himself against the wall as the plane banked slightly.

He glanced at Dan. Sitting there, hands loose, foot tapping away to some tune in his head. So cool. Like always. Will ran his hand over his mouth, glancing for a second out of the plane. Still climbing.

Dan nudged Will, motioned with his head out the door. "Want to change your mind?" he shouted. "Just bail out now."

Will looked, nodded, a whisper of a grin on his face, before he turned away from the open door. Sarah. He'd think about her, forget about the sweat on his upper lip, his hands clenched at his waist, his stomach knotting.

Tom stood up and, putting his hand on the first jumper's shoulder, eased him over to the doorway and into a sitting position. He knelt by his side, whispering to him for a few moments, as he pulled on the static line that snaked to the roof of the plane, where it clipped onto the cable. The jumper shifted a few times, looking up at Tom, who patted his shoulder. The man in the doorway hesitated before he tipped sideways into space.

Dan glanced at Will, smiled, gave him another thumbs-up. Will looked away. He felt sick. Wouldn't it be great if he barfed on Dan's boots?

He heard Dan chanting, "Breathe in. Cool down, breathe."

The second jumper slid into place, waited for instructions, got the pat, and was gone. Will opened his eyes and sat up straighter on the bench.

"Breathe. Cool down. Breathe."

Tom put his hand to his headset for a minute, then slid onto the bench between Dan and Will. He yelled in Dan's ear over the rush of sound from the open doorway. "Wind's up. We have to make another pass. Hang on."

The plane canted to one side and began to climb.

Dan leaned over and repeated what Tom had said. Will nodded. He'd heard.

The plane leveled and Tom waved his thumb at them. It took Will a moment to unclench his hands, to unlock his knees, but finally he stood up, edged to the doorway, and dropped his feet out over the rim of the door. He didn't look at Dan.

"Feel for the footrest, position your hands parallel to the ridges of the step," Tom yelled. Will tried to focus his mind, tried to obey. "Follow the routine, Will, do the routine, slow and sure."

Will looked down at his hand, lined up with the ridges on the edge of the door, not looking at the nothing that lay an inch away from him. Looked at his hand. God, what are you doing to yourself, Spencer?

He felt a hand on his shoulder, heard the jump master yell "Good luck," and then a sharper tap on his shoulder.

He leaned to the left, felt his body hesitate before it fell. Roar, wind past his face, fall, tumble, body twisting out of control. He tried to open his mouth, his eyes, wind pushed everything shut. All he felt was falling, falling, forever.

Roaring stopped, pull on shoulders, lifting, turning,

141

feet dropped, head jerked upright. He opened his eyes. The horizon swung, steadied. He closed his eyes again. He moved one hand, then both, swung a foot. Opened his eyes again. Looked down. *Oh, god.* He shut his eyes again. Worse than he'd dreamed. Don't look down again.

He remembered. Tom told them to check the canopy, see if it had opened all the way. Carefully, he tipped his head, opened his eyes. The chute clouded above him, red and white stripes painful to his eyes in the light.

He felt a stab of pain in his right thigh where the harness bit into his muscle. He put his hands up to the straps and lifted himself carefully, gingerly. His body tipped wildly, and for a moment he thought he was going to fall out of the harness, away from the chute, dropping like a stone.

"Oh, Jesus, just get me down, get me down."

Suddenly he heard a voice, somewhere above him. His name, over and over. He tipped his head again, away from the horizon or the ground, opened his eyes, and looked.

One chute above him, two off to the side. As he watched, one of the jumpers kicked one leg and his entire body spun wildly beneath the chute. Will took a breath. "Oh, no, don't do that." Then he saw it was Dan, pushing at his glasses, waving at him.

"Will!" Dan screamed. "Hey, Will, happy birthday!" Dan tipped his head back and laughed.

Will watched him, remembering how he'd said this was the best part of the jump, the valley and the mountains spread out below him, the peace, the calm, the sense of terror behind him one more time.

Terror behind you. Aw, no. Terror perched on your shoulder, laughing at you. Dan, do you have any idea what you've done?

Sun just up. It struck through the colors of the canopy. He took a deep breath. He knew he had to think about landing, had to get ready. He looked down, then quickly back up. Oh, it was close. Thank you, thank you, almost down, almost over, but he still had to do it right, still had to land without killing himself.

Mountains to the east darkened as the sun slid above them. Below: highway, fields, trees. He shut his eyes. Dan had told him the ground always looked like it was all laid out, ready for him to glide in on the wind like a god to take control. A god. Will took a deep breath, felt a sudden flush of hatred. A god. That's what Dan thought he was. That's why he'd done this, hung him here in mid-space like a goddamned puppet.

Ground was moving faster now, coming up. He grabbed the harness with both hands.

Trees flashing past, highway, house, field, a road, grass and runway, and . . . the ground roared up at him, no time to think, no time to get ready. Roll, they said. Roll. He felt the ground hit his feet, knees, hip, shoulder, as his body twisted. He heard the parachute sigh down behind him. He lay facedown in the dirt, breathing, feeling the earth under his body, the whole length of it. He didn't want to move. Didn't want to move.

143

"Hey, Will. You OK?"

He didn't move.

"Will?" Dan's voice rose, got closer. "Will!"

Will sat up, swiveled on his knees, began to pull the harness off his shoulders.

"Shit, man, you had me scared for a minute. You didn't move for the longest time. I landed and there you were, facedown in the mud." Dan pounded him on the back, then stopped to gather in the cloth of his parachute. "Wasn't that great? Didn't I tell you?" As he helped Will unbuckle the harness, he started to laugh. "Hey, your hands are still shaking."

"I can do it. Let it alone." Will turned away. He had to get away from Dan's chattering.

"Beautiful. Wasn't it beautiful?" Dan pulled the chute out behind Will, fluffing it in the breeze. "You want to do it again? I'll buy you another jump. My treat."

Will whirled. "I said let it alone, Dan. Leave the god-damned chute alone. Leave me alone." He hated it that his voice was shaking, too.

"What?"

"Just leave me alone. I'll do it." Will pulled the silk out of Dan's hands.

"What's wrong?"

"That wasn't beautiful, that was awful, so just—just leave me alone for a minute so I can . . ." He leaned over, hands on his knees, breathing in frantic gulps, the parachute billowing out around him.

144

Dan didn't move. He stood, hands loose at his sides. "You OK?"

Will straightened, unzipped the jumpsuit, pulling it off his shoulders, and stepped out of it. He balled it up, threw it on top of the parachute that was now soaking into the wet ground at his feet, and took off across the soggy field, slipping a little in the mud at the side of the runway.

"Hey, wait!" He heard Dan's voice, footsteps behind him. He ran faster toward the fence. A Jeep passed him. The one Dan told him would come out to pick him up and everybody would stand around and slap him on the back and tell him how great he did.

He reached the fence and ran along it to the opening and through it and toward his truck. He heard Dan call his name again. He reached into his pocket for the keys and was at the door of the truck when Dan pulled him around from behind.

"Hey, stop being a jerk."

Will hit Dan's arm away, then hit him in the chest with both hands, knocking him against a car door. Dan stood for a second, his hands flat at his sides, staring, mouth open.

Will gulped, trying to get his breath.

"God, what is your problem, Spencer?"

"You are. So let's do it. Right here."

Dan pushed himself off the car and swung at Will, hitting him right below the nose. Will felt his head whip

145

back and his nose pop. Dizzy pain shot up and over his head, and he gagged, covering his nose with his hand. Blood in his mouth, stinging his lips. Dan hunched over his hand, fingers spread in front of him. He raised his head and Will swung. He missed, but swung with the other hand and felt it smash into Dan's jaw. Dan hit the car again and before he could pull himself upright he slid to the ground.

Will watched him go down, then more pain hit him, this time up his arm. He grabbed his wrist with the other hand and stepped over Dan's legs to the water faucet on the side of the hangar and turned it on full force. He cupped water in his good hand and splashed it over the other, then brought it to his face, groaning as the cold hit his nose.

Dan shook his head as if he was trying to clear his eyes. "Crap," he muttered.

Will went to the back of the truck, found a rag, and after he'd soaked it in the water, gave it to Dan, and waited while he wrapped it around his hand and held it to his face.

"Jesus, you didn't have to hit so hard," Dan muttered.

He looked like he could pass out here on the hot pavement.

"OK, Dan." Will spoke. Get it out. You've hit him for the first time in your life. So finish the job. He looked down at Dan. "If we're going to fight, we might as well know why."

Will concentrated on looking at Dan, not looking away

146

even once. "I hate you for making me jump. You forced me into it. I thought I was going to die every minute I was up there. And you thought it was a big joke. Great big present you gave me. Scared the shit out of me."

Will unclenched his hand, feeling the bones move under the skin. He felt nauseated. He took a breath so he could go on.

"But I shouldn't be surprised, should I?" He looked down at Dan. "Should I? That's the way it's always been between you and me. Dan giving the orders and me, good old Will, trailing along, doing what he's told. Like some dumb dog that can't think for himself."

Dan looked up at him through his crooked glasses, playing with the rag wrapped around his hand.

"You know how you wanted me to do that paper for Quinn? How you said you'd help me with it? We'd work together, like always, you said? Do you really believe we ever worked together on things?" Will leaned toward Dan, feeling his head throb as he moved.

"It was never like that! You always did the work and then I came along and put my name on it. All those book reports and maps and papers. And you'd say, 'Good job, Will,' and we both knew that was a crock because *I* hadn't done anything. It was all *you*." Will pointed at Dan, his finger rigid. "Maybe it made *you* feel good, but it made me feel like shit."

"Will, this is crazy. Stop it."

"No, you shut up and listen." He took another breath before he could go on. "This jump was just the same thing all over again. It was to make you feel good. To show what a great friend you are. Nothing about me." He shook his head and shifted, his hands at his belt, keeping him upright. "I was scared worse than I'd ever been and it was all for you."

He felt another wave of nausea and he leaned against the warm side of the truck.

"I tried to tell you to lay off, but you never got the picture. Well, I'm sick of trying to explain myself." He was breathing hard, between every word.

"You made a big deal of it being my birthday. So you know what I want for my birthday? For you to leave me alone, OK? This was it." He pointed out at the airfield. "That's it, buddy. No more."

"Wait. You can't just—"

"Don't tell me I can't. Never again. *Don't tell me what to do ever again!*"

He turned away toward the back of the truck, suddenly afraid he would cry. He bent over the truckbed until he could go on. "Jesus, why did you make this so hard?" He looked over his shoulder at Dan. "Why did I have to hit you to make you listen to me?" His voice cracked and he wiped at his face with his sleeve.

Dan stared at him a minute, then pushed himself slowly off the ground. He stood with one hand on the hood of the car, looking down at the ground. Finally he straightened his glasses, turned slowly, and walked away.

Will stood listening to his own breathing, shaky, shallow gasps, as he watched Dan go.

CHAPTER SIXTEEN

Enlisting

Ten o'clock. The center didn't open until ten o'clock. Will edged his hands down his pant legs. Fifteen minutes. He glanced at the papers on the dashboard of the truck. Everything there he needed. Everything Joe had said he would need.

He glanced around the parking lot. He'd be first in line. No one else here beating down the door.

Last day of classes. He'd gone to school early to hand in the paper to Quinn and told him he wouldn't be in class today. Quinn just nodded. Too shocked to say anything, probably. He wouldn't get to see Dan's face when he saw the paper, but that didn't matter now. Neither did the two tests he was missing today. He'd graduate . . . barely. That was all he needed. That's what Joe said.

149

It was lucky Joe was home last night. He'd needed someone to tell him how to do this, someone who wasn't Dan. And Joe had outlined every step . . . checking out of school so he'd have the papers, who to see here, what to ask for, all the first steps.

Joe was good to talk to, real straight with him. Didn't ask a million questions.

Didn't ask . . . why all of a sudden.

Why all of a sudden?

He took a deep breath. He didn't have to answer to anybody. So long as he knew the answer.

Did he know the answer?

Maybe.

Just remember hanging there under that parachute like a puppet.

Yesterday wasn't the first time he'd felt like those little kids in that old book about Pinocchio. He'd always hated the picture of that old man and all the little kids hanging there. The old guy pulls a string, the arm goes up.

Someone tells Will to do something, Will does it.

Dan tells Will to do something, Will does it.

Right. That was it.

And Dan was why he was here today, why he didn't wait until after graduation, why he asked Joe not to tell anyone. He'd been so mad yesterday he was sweating, but it wasn't at Dan. It was at himself for letting Dan do this to him again. And when he hit Dan, it was because it was the only way he could get it over with. He couldn't just calmly tell Dan anything and make it stick. He'd tried

150

that. So he had to blow the whole thing, beat Dan up.

It had worked.

But, oh man, he hated the way Dan had looked at him yesterday. That was bad.

Don't think about that. Think about what you're going to say in there in a few minutes.

He crossed his arms on the steering wheel, resting his head against them. This wasn't getting any easier. Not after thinking about it all day yesterday and all night. None of it was any easier. The only time he'd been sure about anything was when he lay there on the ground yesterday and decided he was getting out. That was the only time he was sure of anything. Even talking to Joe last night, he kept wanting to call up Dan and ask if he was doing the right thing.

He looked at his watch, rubbed it for a minute. This was probably a dumbass thing to be doing too. He could just hear Dan.

"You'll get your head blown off. Serve you right."

Dan's voice filled the truck.

No, remember what Joe said . . . all the reasons. Good training, money for school, serving your country.

He wiped his hands on his jeans again, then blew his hair off his forehead. He nodded. Yeah, good reasons. Are you listening, Dan? He clenched his fist on his knee. Dan doesn't matter. You don't have to convince him, so long as you're sure.

He checked his watch again.

Five more minutes. Third period. He always met Sarah

after this class, in the hall between his English and her algebra.

So what will you tell Sarah?

Wait for me. I'll come back and we'll take up where we left off.

Whenever he thought of Sarah, he got the shakes inside. Just when it was all starting to happen with her, it would be over. And she was most of the reason he didn't want to be a puppet anymore. He'd done the paper for her. He'd even thought of writing "To Sarah" on the first page like they do in books, so she wouldn't look at him the way she did that night in the library when she'd told him not to let Dan run his life, so she'd look at him the way she did up on the hill when he kissed her.

He could think about that the rest of the morning. Not a good way to get him inside that building.

Time? 10:01. Give them time to get set up, get their uniforms on straight and their pens uncapped.

Oh, boy.

He knew all the reasons, he'd memorized them, he could recite them. He was doing this on his own, nobody pushing him around.

But right now he wished he was sitting in English and when the bell rang he could walk out in that hall and hold hands with Sarah and wait for Dan to come tell him where they were going for lunch.

He got out of the truck and headed for the building.

CHAPTER SEVENTEEN

Noon on the Hill

Sarah wasn't surprised to see Will outside the door of the chemistry lab. And because she had seen Dan's face last night and heard his story of the fight, she wasn't surprised at the way Will looked, his swollen nose and cracked knuckles. As they pulled out of the parking lot, she told him he looked better than Dan did.

"But, then, I'm not real objective," she said, hoping he would smile.

He did briefly, without looking at her. The red soreness of his nose and hands made her knees hurt, and as they headed up the hill, she noticed his hands shaking as he sipped at the coffee he'd bought at the drugstore. Funny—now that she'd touched his face, run her fingers over his eyebrows and down the tip of his nose, she noticed his face differently, how tired his eyes looked, how the sweat collected in bright beads just below his curls.

"Where're we going?"

"I thought back up to our hill." He did look at her then, just quickly. "I have something to tell you."

She looked back out the window, feeling a sudden cold spot inside her.

He reached over and squeezed her hand. "Don't worry, Sar. It will be all right."

So she knew something was coming.

He drove up the foothills to the stretch of sagebrush where they'd come the night of the prom, and when they got out of the truck, into the hot noon, the sun bounced up from the valley into their eyes. Sarah pulled herself up on a rock, folded her legs under her, and watched Will, who didn't sit, but leaned against the truck, picking a sprig of sagebrush, spinning it between his fingers, flipping a pebble up the side of the hill. Finally he turned around and told her what he had done.

As he talked, she sat without moving, but as she realized what he was saying, she suddenly felt dizzy. The longer he talked, the more she felt she would faint, so she put her head down on her knees and waited until she could speak.

"Why?" she asked.

None of his answers made sense; nothing he said, all the reasons he rolled out so easily, made any sense at all until she felt such a wave of anger, she knew she had to get away for a minute to get control of herself. She slid off the rock, stood a minute blinking in the heat, and then scrambled up the hill behind them, slipping on the loose rocks, grabbing oak branches and sagebrush until she was far enough away, behind a boulder, standing in the cool of its shadow, and she could lean her head against it and let go, gasps of breath and tears, fists jammed into her cheeks, forehead pressed so hard into the rock that it hurt.

Enlisting. Joining the army. Ready to fight for his country. Get away. Need it for himself. All the things he had said spun in her head and in her mouth as she repeated them, trying to make them line up in some kind of order.

Hadn't he been paying attention?

Did he think all the things she had said about the war had been a joke, a game?

How could he make himself a part of all of that? How could he *choose* to do it?

She looked down the hill to where he sat, back to her, hair bright in the sun, staring out over the valley.

"Damn it, damn it, damn him, damn everybody."

She unclenched her fists, rubbed her hands together, and when they stopped shaking, searched in her skirt pocket for a Kleenex.

How could he do this to her?

She steadied herself against the rock for another minute.

She knew what it was. He was getting back at Dan for the jump. And *she* didn't matter to him at all, no matter

155

what he'd said and done the past few days. He didn't care what she thought so long as he could make a point to Dan, get back at Dan, get away from Dan.

What about her?

She took a long, shaky breath.

He'd said he respected the way she felt about the war, but that he didn't see it that way. How could anyone believe it was right? How could anyone read the stuff she handed out every day and want to be part of it? Trouble was, he hadn't read it. He couldn't have. He was joining up not knowing what was happening over there. They'd won. The generals and Nixon and all those people Dad thought were so right had won if they'd gotten to Will.

So forget her. Forget everything that had happened.

Damn, damn, damn.

They didn't talk on the drive back to her house. Out of the corner of her eye she could see Will looking at her and knew he wanted to talk. But she wouldn't. It was over and done. He'd done it. Without asking or discussing it with her. So let him live with it.

She tightened her hands into a knot in her lap.

She'd start crying if she had to say another word. And she wouldn't give him that satisfaction.

As he started to pull up the drive, she opened the car door. "Let me out here."

"Sarah . . ."

She got out and slammed the door behind her, but stopped, her hand resting flat on the smooth metal.

"Sarah, can't we talk about this?"

She shook her head.

"Why not?"

"What's there to say?" She didn't look at him.

"What?"

"There's nothing left to say. You did this without talking about it with . . . anyone. So it's too late now."

"I'm leaving day after tomorrow. I want to see you before I go. I don't want to go with things like this, Sarah."

She squeezed her eyes shut against the tears, her hand clenched over the top of the half-open window. Suddenly she felt his hand over hers, and before he could say anything else or make her look at him, she jerked her hand away and ran up the drive to the house.

She didn't go right in, but walked around the house, kicking at the grass, her face sore from tears. She felt panicked, as if she had to do something, but had no idea what, as if something awful was happening and she had to stop it.

Leaning against the dog run, she pushed her hair back. "Sure, Sarah, as if you can do *anything*," she said. "As if anything *you* do can make any difference at all." She felt one of the dogs lick her fingers through the wire mesh, and sliding down to the ground, she covered her face and sobbed.

They'd cut his hair and stick him in a uniform.

And that was just the start.

Dan was sitting at the kitchen table, newspaper, bread, peanut butter, spread out around him. He looked up at her. "Where have *you* been?"

"Out." Through the door she saw the top of her father's head over the newspaper. News was on. "Where's Mom?"

"At the store. She said dinner would be at six." He looked up at her. "What's with you?"

She stopped. "I saw Will."

He opened a section of the paper and propped it against the glass of milk. "Yeah?" He smoothed peanut butter across a slice of bread.

"He's going into the army."

"Yeah, right." He looked up at her. "He told you that?"

"He's done it. He's leaving day after tomorrow."

He set down the knife and pushed the plate away from him, staring at her. "No, he didn't. Don't joke about—"

"You think I'm joking? Here." Sarah reached behind her to the phone, yanked the receiver off the hook, and held it out to him. "Call him. Ask him!"

"He wouldn't—"

"Yes, he would. He did. And there's nothing you can do about it," she shouted, slamming the receiver down. "Nothing anyone can do about it."

"What's going on?"

As she went to the sink and turned on the water, she

heard the sudden quiet as their father turned off the television. "There's so much noise I can't hear the news." He stood in the doorway.

Sarah glanced at him and then turned on the tap, filled a glass, and swallowed half of it. Too bad, she thought, but said over her shoulder, "Ask Dan."

"Sarah says Will's enlisted in the army. I don't believe it." Dan twisted to look at her. "That's a bad joke, Sarah. He wouldn't do it just like that."

"Well, he did. And he didn't ask you, did he? He didn't ask any of us. He just went out and did it. To get back at you for making him jump."

"You're full of it, Sarah."

"So ask him. He wouldn't do anything so stupid otherwise."

"Be quiet, both of you!" Dad slammed his hand down on the counter. He looked at Sarah. "When is he leaving?"

"Day after tomorrow."

Sarah saw Dan close his eyes and lean back from the table.

"Good for Will." Their father nodded his head. "I'm proud of him. We need young men like Will."

"To do what? Fill your June quota?" Dan's chair bumped against the stove as he lurched to his feet. "Isn't that why he's leaving so soon? Because you can't draft people quickly enough? You don't need people like Will. All you need is bodies."

Their father straightened. "I will not have that kind of talk from you."

"Well, I don't want to listen to how proud you are of Will. That's just so much—"

"I am proud of anyone willing to serve his country. You should be, too."

"Why? Because he didn't wait to be drafted? Because he was stupid enough to enlist?"

"You watch what you say, young man. There are limits—"

"Limits to what, Dad? Have I lost my right to free speech? Is that going to go next? So the President can go on with his immoral war without any opposition?"

Sarah held up her hand, shaking her head. "Dan, stop it."

"That would be easier, wouldn't it? Just lock up—"

"It's not a question of —"

"Be quiet and listen, both of you. Listen!" Sarah screamed the last word and they stopped, both leaning toward each other across the room, faces rigid. "Listen to yourselves. I can't stand this. Here you both are, buried in newspapers and TV news, and all you can do is argue with each other about this. And Will . . . You're not thinking about Will. Neither of you are. No one is."

"What's there to say? Will said it all." Dan's mouth twisted. "He couldn't make it clearer if he spit in my face."

"He didn't *do* anything to *you*. And if you'd just stop thinking of yourself for one second, you'd see he did it to himself."

She turned. "Dad, you talk about how great it is he's

160

going to serve his country. This is *Will*, Daddy. It's not just some recruit. It's someone you know. Doesn't that make any difference?"

Her father shook his head. "It can't. I have to be ready to send anyone, even my own son, if I have to." He touched his fingertips to the table, looking down, not at her. "Fortunately, that's not necessary."

"You're damn straight it isn't necessary. You won't catch me doing anything so stupid." Dan picked up the sack of bread from the table and threw it onto the counter, grabbed his keys off the hook, and headed for the door.

"Right, Dan." Sarah stepped toward him. "You're lucky. You can just talk about how you're against the war. Not a lot of risk in doing that, is there?"

"He didn't have to enlist. He could have—"

"Oh, sure, I know. He could have gone to college with you. But how long would he have lasted there? You know Will. He wouldn't make it. And he didn't want to do that. So he decided to face things."

"Is that what he's doing? You call running out and enlisting in the damned army facing things? Where's your big opposition to the war all of a sudden?"

"I don't know, Dan. That's why I . . . I was awful to Will when he told me." She stopped and suddenly she had to sit down. She was crying again, awful aching sobs. "It's still there. It's the way I feel. But it's not the way Will feels. And I've got to . . . He's got to do things for himself. Even if I don't agree with him."

"So suddenly it's OK to go in the army, if that's the

way you feel," Dan said, mockingly. He lifted his hands and shrugged. "Pretty pathetic, if you ask me."

"No, you know what *is* pathetic?" She grabbed a towel and scrubbed her face, looking up at him. "You are. If you're so right about the war, why don't you do more than talk about it? You made fun of me and Kris when we handed out buttons. Like you're above all that, too good to actually *do* anything. I sometimes think this whole thing is just an excuse to argue with Dad, not anything you really believe in."

She stood up, hands tight around the towel.

"I really blew it with Will this afternoon, but at least I know I'm doing something about what I think is important. So is Will. So is Dad." She flung her hand at her father, where he stood, arms folded, watching them.

"What about you, Dan? Or are you just good at talking?"

He looked back at her, his jaw working, but he didn't blink, didn't turn away. The three of them stood without speaking until Sarah looked down at the mess on the table, the crumbs, the dirty knife, the parts of the newspaper on the floor and the table. "I have to get out of here."

She left them standing in the kitchen, and as she headed out the door up the slope to the dog run, she wondered who would leave the room first.

She unhooked the latch of the gate to the dog run and let the dogs out, let them jump at her and gallop out across the lawn toward Dad's garden. She headed up the hill away from the house, the noise, the words from Dan and her father.

She thought about the first time she and Will had held each other against the cold. While she climbed the trail to the mouth of the canyon, that's all she could think of; she couldn't move beyond that.

By the time she reached the cutoff to Malan's Peak, she could make herself put it all together, see him with his hair cut, wearing a uniform, one of the soldiers on the news on TV, one of the soldiers blowing up Vietnam.

But those pictures kept sliding out of focus. And as she climbed toward Castle Rock, she remembered the night they had danced on the hillside to "A Whiter Shade of Pale," galoshes loose on her feet, Spearmint clean on his breath, his hands touching her face and his fingers tangling in her hair, his mouth on her cheek, and when he kissed her his breath running sweet clear to her toes.

CHAPTER EIGHTEEN

Jump #11

Four other jumpers sat on the benches with Dan; a club, Tom had said, going jumping on a dare.

Dan repositioned the helmet on his head. On a dare. Stupid. As if this was any place to play games. He leaned back against the seat and shut his eyes. But if they hadn't been going up today, he wouldn't be here. Tom wouldn't have taken the plane up just for him.

Asphalt boiled outside the plane as it rolled down the runway, heat bounced off the runway, light glared off the wings. Behind his eyes, the sun was melting his brain.

Once he got out in the air he'd feel better. He could already feel the rush as the wind hit him, as he opened his arms to catch the lift. If he could just make it until then, he'd be OK. After last night he needed time to think, to clear his head. Up here, away from everybody, maybe everything would come clear.

He stretched out his legs until they bumped into those of one of the men. He looked up and the guy smiled at him and winked. Dan looked away. He felt a tap on his shoulder.

"You done this before?"

Dan nodded.

"How many times?"

"Ten."

The guy whistled and turned to the other men and shouted, "This kid has jumped ten times!" He held up both hands, fingers wide, and waved them in front of his face.

Another tap on his shoulder. "Is it fun?"

Dan nodded, shutting his eyes and folding his arms. He heard the man yell to his friends, "He says it's fun!" Dan heard them all laugh. Suddenly he wanted to get this jump over with. Today all he wanted was for the plane to stop climbing, for Tom to get rid of the other jumpers, so he could jump.

He looked at the gray shell of the plane, cables and straps for the chutes, the open door of the plane, the men shouting to each other, laughing and pulling at their gear. Half scared, half excited.

Like the news story from inside that helicopter in Vietnam. Same feeling. That twist between Let's get this over with and Let's put it off forever.

Will was heading for this. In six months he'd be sitting in a chopper with a bunch of GIs, ready to pour out into a village already smoking from the bombs the jets had dropped. A village with all the huts on fire and old people trying to pull stuff out of the way and animals and kids running in circles, bellowing and screaming, trying to get away from the guns and the smoke and the explosions. And GIs tying up VC prisoners, twisting their arms back, pushing them down into the mud. Prisoners who looked like the kids. Dan shook his head. Too much television. Stuff was getting to him.

But it wasn't just TV, it was happening. And now when he watched Uncle Walter, he'd be looking for Will pointing a gun in the face of some ten-year-old kid or standing in some hole in the ground, hip deep in mud, telling jokes for the camera.

God, what made Will decide to do this? Had he been planning it all along and just not said anything? Was that why all the talk about not going to college, to get Dan ready for this? Or had he decided when he punched Dan in the face? Had he loved that so much that he decided to join up and do it for real?

Dan rubbed his face. No way. No matter what had happened between them, he knew it had to be hard for Will to hit him. It sure wasn't going to be easy for him to torch some old lady's house.

Pushing up his glasses, he leaned his head against the side of the plane. All that awful sadness he'd been seeing for years was going to land on top of Will, and there wasn't a thing anyone could do to change it. Not Sarah with her peace pamphlets or Dad with his rah-rah for democracy. Nobody. Will would just have to get used to it.

He tightened one of the harness straps and pulled a little on the helmet. The plane had pretty well leveled out, so they'd be there soon. He glanced at the other jumpers. They were all quiet now, staring out the open door of the plane, one licking his lips, one smiling.

Will would have to get used to whatever was out there.

Just like Dan had had to get used to sitting in that doorway, freezing wind slapping him in the face and a big gray nothing right below his feet.

Tom got up from the bench and crouched in front of the three men, steadying himself with one hand to the floor, talking to them, going over procedure again. Dan watched for a minute, then looked away.

Will had said he hated Dan for making him jump.

But Will had faked it. He'd gone along with Dan until he landed. Just like Dan had done that first jump. He'd wanted to tell Dad to get out of his room and leave him alone. "Thank you very much for your birthday present but you can take it and stuff it."

But instead, he'd leaped out of bed, jumped into his clothes, and trotted out to the car after Dad. Doing what he was told. Faking it the whole time. Until he'd done it so many times it didn't scare him anymore, until his stomach stopped curling, and he didn't have falling dreams the night before. Until he'd done more jumps

167

than Dad. That was when the joy started. When he'd beaten Dad.

So did Will enlist to get back at him?

No one was that crazy.

Maybe Will wanted to stop faking it. Maybe he'd found something more important than just going along.

So, what about you, Dan? Is jumping out of planes to prove something to Dad the only thing that matters to you?

Wasn't that what Sarah meant when she said he was pathetic? that he didn't take risks?

Hey, jumping out of a plane was a risk.

Only if it scared him. And it hadn't done that for a long time.

So what does scare you, Ulvang?

He took a breath. Him. Always him. Standing up to the man. Telling him, no, *I* won't do what you tell me, I won't follow your plan anymore or play by your rules. I'm thinking for myself now. And I think the war is wrong. And . . . and what? What came next?

The first jumper got up, followed the routine at the doorway, and was gone, followed quickly by the second. Dan wiped his hands on his knees, then higher across his chest and down his stomach.

"God, it's coming," he thought. "Breathe in, cool down . . ."

Will could die over there. He could be one of those faces in *Life* magazine.

The third jumper disappeared.

168

"Ready, Dan?" Tom's face was in front of his, too close almost to focus.

Dan pushed up on his glasses, set his hands on the bench beside him, and stood up. Everything inside seemed to lurch and then settle heavily.

He moved to the doorway, not looking out, and squatted by the door.

"Hey, ease up!" Tom yelled in his ear.

Dan lifted his head, feeling Tom's grip on his arm. "Let go!" Tom yelled, and pulled Dan's hand off his shoulder. "You about took my arm off. You OK?"

Dan wiped his upper lip, nodding. "Yeah, OK."

"We're almost there. Get into position."

Dan looked at his legs, tried to make his feet move into place on the ledge outside the door, tried to inch his body closer to the edge. Nothing happened, as if connection between thoughts and body had been cut.

"I . . ." he said, then looked up at Tom.

Tom shook him slightly on the shoulder, frowning at him. "Dan? You with me?"

Dan nodded, mouthed, "Sure."

He swung his legs into position, settled his helmet, pushed up his glasses, set his hands. He glanced to his left, out at space, and his stomach rioted. He closed his eyes.

Breathe, breathe, breathe.

What do I do now?

Tom tapped him on the shoulder. "Go!"

He tipped sideways, felt himself falling. He tried to

focus on positon, but couldn't feel his hands and feet. He had to get into position, to hold himself in place. He tried to focus, tried to get it all together. But it wasn't working and he felt his body twist and spin. He was out of control.

He hadn't been counting. He didn't know how long it had been. He was falling too fast, it was time. He brought his hand to his chest, felt for the handle, pulled, and felt the lift on his shoulders and body as the chute opened above him.

He sucked in a breath, heard it snarl in his throat, looked up to check the chute. His body tipped a little and he felt a spurt of nausea.

He looked out at the horizon, like they said to do when you felt sick, took deep breaths. It didn't help. The horizon was out of place, too far away, the ground so far below it was out of focus.

He tipped his head back, eyes closed. He couldn't look out anymore. This was as bad as the first time he'd jumped. It was like that, only worse.

"Dan, Dan, heads up, landing, landing, Dan, do you hear me?"

Dan shook his head, put a hand to his helmet. "What? Oh, Christ!" Ground rushing at him, too late to adjust his fall, just enough time to get ready, to try to miss the runway, think about landing.

Ground came up fast, and just at the last minute it switched from brown to gray and no way to adjust, he hit the runway and toppled, hands hitting the hard surface, scraping skin off into the grit, and then his left foot twisted against the ground, and when he tried to stand up his foot jangled and his leg folded under him.

He eased himself down onto the blacktop and took off his helmet. He'd finally figured it all out. He had to crash and burn to do it, but he'd figured it out. He closed his eyes, his shoulders sagging. He needed to sit here a minute and then he'd be ready.

CHAPTER NINETEEN

Graduation

He had a long wait in the emergency room. The doctor on call was at lunch, and since Dan wasn't dying, they let him sit while the guy finished his sandwich. It didn't matter, Dan thought. He hurt everywhere else, why should his foot be different? He touched his jaw and his hand. He was a mess. In two days he'd been hurt more than in all the rest of his life put together. Well, there's always a first time.

After the doctor had taped his ankle and given him a prescription for pain medication, he called home and asked Mom to come get him. She didn't panic, just sounded relieved that "hurt" meant only a sprained ankle. On the ride home, he told her that he wasn't going to jump anymore.

"Why?"

He shrugged. "I've done it enough."

She didn't say anything for a while, and then she asked, "Didn't you have graduation practice today?"

"Yeah."

"Why didn't you go?"

He let out a gust of air. "I just couldn't go in and hang around with everyone. Like everything is normal."

"It isn't, is it?"

He shook his head. "Not quite."

He looked at her. "I'm not going to make graduation tonight either, Mom. Sorry."

She tightened her lips, nodding. But she didn't say anything.

Oh damn, he thought.

After turning up the drive and parking close to the house, she looked across at him. "Can you get out?"

"Mom, I need to talk to Dad as soon as he gets home. I want to rest for a while, but tell him, will you, that I need to see him?"

She ran her hand around the steering wheel. "Anything you can tell me?"

He hesitated a moment and then shook his head. "Sorry, Mom. I have to talk to him alone."

She reached over and ran her fingers down the side of his face. "OK, Dan."

She didn't say any more, just helped him into the house and onto his bed, where she propped his ankle on a pillow, left a glass of water and the medicine by the side of the bed, and shut his door.

He knew he couldn't sleep, but he shut his eyes and tried to ignore the throbbing of his ankle. It didn't work, and finally he gave up and took one of the pills. At least it relaxed him for a little, made everything stop spinning. For the first time in two days he felt tired.

When he woke up, the room was dark. He sat up quickly, but fell back as the pain hit him. "Oh, shit, I forgot."

He lay still until the throbbing stopped, then swung his legs over the edge of the bed, straightened his glasses, and stood up.

"OK, Dan," he whispered, "here we go."

The house was quiet and it wasn't until he hobbled into the living room that he saw his father standing in the kitchen, reading the paper by the light over the sink. He folded the paper when he saw Dan.

"There's the sky diver. How you doing?"

"I'm OK, Dad."

"You're sure? How bad is it?"

"Not too." Dan shook his head. "I landed wrong."

"There's always a first time."

"Yeah." Dan winced as he put too much weight on his foot. Funny you should say that, he thought.

"Come on, sit down."

"No."

His father paused, long fingers running along the counter. Dan's breathing quickened and he felt sweat under his clothes. He could count the throbs of pain in his foot. They matched his heartbeat. Like a massive bruise down there.

"Dad, I probably should try to explain this to you, but it wouldn't make any difference. Anyway, we've said it all by now."

"What are you talking about?"

Dan reached into his wallet and, opening it, took out his draft card. "About this."

He ran his finger along the edges of the card, then held it out to his father. "I'm turning this in to you. I refuse to carry it any longer."

His father stared at him, blue eyes cold and unmoving. Dan pushed up his glasses. "Dan, you know what this means. So I am just going to forget what you have said here and when you feel better we'll talk."

"No, no more talk. No more words. This is it."

"This is foolishness. This is not a game to play. This is a matter of life and death here."

"I know. It wouldn't matter otherwise."

"So . . . Will leaves and you throw everything away. Is that it?"

Dan felt himself swaying a little and he reached for the counter to steady himself. "Just take the card."

"There are other ways."

"Not any I can handle."

His father stared at him, standing so still, as if he was holding everything under tight control. He spoke quietly.

"You want so much to face the world on your own.

It's out there . . . just waiting for you." His mouth tightened. "I have never found it easy to express feelings. You know that. But I know, Dan, that nothing is easy. That you have to be hard." He raised his fist in front of his chest. "Hard as nails to face things. And if you do this, hard doesn't begin to describe how things will be for you. Are you ready for that?"

Dan nodded. "Yes." He felt the breath inside him, as if he would explode, but he was afraid to move enough even to breathe, as he watched his father's face.

"*Think* about this."

"I have." Dan clenched the card, bending it, holding it out to his father. "Here, take it."

"No, I won't help you."

Shifting against the counter to brace himself, Dan took the card in both hands and tore it in two pieces. He put the pieces on the counter beside him.

His father stared at the torn draft card.

"I'm sorry, Dad."

Finally Dan pulled himself up straight, waited until he knew his foot would support him, and walked out of the room.

CHAPTER TWENTY

Night at the Trailhead

Will sat in his bedroom looking at the bare walls and clean desktop. Mom hadn't wanted him to put everything away, but he needed to do it, needed to feel he didn't have a place he could come back to.

He needed a clean break.

The officer at the recruitment center told him that until he passed the physical and took the oath tomorrow, he could still change his mind. If he got that far, he'd be safe. The rest would be a breeze.

He'd survived telling Mom he wasn't going to graduation tonight. That was hard. She'd wanted to go and clap for the first person in the family to graduate from high school.

But he couldn't face that. Go up there and take the

diploma from Mr. Wilson—no questions about how he got it. How little he'd learned to get it. How badly he'd done. Or who helped him. With Dan sitting there watching.

And Sarah.

Reaching into his jeans pockets, he pulled out a stick of gum, unwrapped it, and twisted it into his mouth.

After tomorrow a whole bunch of new people would be telling him what to do every minute of his life. But . . . that's the way he wanted it.

Hard to believe it was all over.

He thought of Mike's stupid rhyme: "No more homework, no more books, no more teachers' . . ."

No more feeling like he'd swallowed his tongue when a teacher called on him. No more feeling like a first-class jerk when he failed a test. Or got a D on a paper that Dan had said was a cinch. No more walking into a classroom feeling like throwing up because he knew he'd blow it again today.

No more Dan. Or Sarah.

He leaned back against the wall and whispered it. "No more Sarah."

How does that feel?

Like someone just told him he couldn't laugh anymore.

No one told you to do this, Will. You did it yourself.

Right.

So don't expect anyone to like it. Especially her.

He lay back on the bed, hands crossed under his head, and shut his eyes.

After his father left the house, left without speaking to anyone, Dan stood alone in his dark room, listening to the quiet of the house. After half an hour he went out back, hobbling along on his crutches, and he found Sarah sitting on the grass with the dogs on either side of her, just out of the light from the back door.

She asked how his foot felt and told him that Mom had gone to a friend's house.

"Weren't you supposed to usher at graduation?"

She nodded. "I called Mrs. Lee and told her I was sick." She hunched over her knees. "I couldn't do it."

"So Will was all by himself to graduate."

She nodded.

Then she said, "I heard you and Dad."

He waited for her to go on.

"I'm glad," she said very quietly.

"Yeah?" He pulled himself up on the crutches to ease his shoulders.

"I'll help you. Any way I can," she said, a little louder.

"Thanks, baby sister." He peered down at her, sitting there with her arms wrapped around her legs, hair tangled around her face.

"What will happen now?"

He took a deep breath. "I don't know. It's up to Dad."

He heard her take a breath. "You know what he'll do."

He nodded. "Yes."

She didn't say any more, and finally he said, "I'm going to call Will. You want to see him?"

She pulled up a bunch of grass and dropped it on her shoe. He couldn't see her face, the way her cheek was pressed into her knees, but he could see her nod. Then she looked up at him. "You going to tell him what you did?"

"Yeah."

She turned her face away again.

"I'll call at ten. He should be back from graduation by then."

After a minute, he heard her say, "OK."

They waited at the trailhead, as far as they got before Dan's foot gave out. He sagged against a rock, trying to find a position for his foot so it wouldn't hurt.

Will had said he'd be right out. Funny, he hadn't said much when Dan told him what he'd done to his draft card. Just whistled and said, "Geez, Dan, you do things the hard way."

As if he knew another way.

The silence roared around them until Dan started hearing scrambles and rustles from the scrub oak on either side of the trail. A jumble of milky clouds skidded around the moon. Sarah sat off to the side, looking down the trail.

When the truck turned up the drive at the house, she stood up. Soon Dan heard footsteps and saw a glimmer of light from Will's shirt.

"Hey, Will," Dan called. "Over here."

"Hi." Will's voice came out of the dark and then Dan

saw him, hands shoved in his pockets, shoulders hunched. "Well, here we are."

"Yeah." Dan pushed up his glasses. He could see Will's face clearly in the moonlight and see that Will was looking at Sarah.

She had turned away, facing the dark clumps of scrub oak at the side of the trail, her arms crossed tightly in front of her. After a minute, Dan heard her let out a long breath and she turned toward Will, who stepped across the trail to her. They stood together, not touching.

Crickets surrounded them with sound.

"Sorry about your foot," said Will, after a while.

"Yeah, well, had to happen, I guess. It was dumb." Dan puffed out his cheeks. "You're leaving tomorrow?"

"Yeah." Will pushed at a rock with his foot. "I'll be stationed at Fort Ord in California."

"Hey, you can go surfing. We always said we'd do that, remember?"

"Right."

"You beat me to it."

"I guess."

"Will, I messed up. I'm sorry." Everything. So much.

"You weren't the only one."

"Yes, I was."

"You want to fight about it?"

"No." Dan slumped against the rock.

Sarah reached up to smooth a strand of hair off her face, and Dan saw Will watching her. After a minute he looked at Dan. "So what happens to you now?" he asked.

181

Dan eased his foot down to the ground, trying his weight on it. "I'm not sure. I'll have to get a lawyer and find out, I guess. From what I read, I guess it'll take a while. These things go slowly."

"You scared?"

Dan nodded. "Hell yes." He shifted on the rock, stretching out his leg. "But that's OK."

"Let me know what's going on, will you?"

"Sure."

No one spoke. Finally Will said, "I gotta go. I leave at five A.M."

Dan pushed himself off the rock. "I'll come down the trail with you."

"No, I'll be OK. You stay here." Will put out his hand. "See you, Dan."

"Take it easy." They shook hands, reaching across the trail to each other.

"Yeah. Like always." Will turned to Sarah, and Dan watched as he put his hand on her arm, slid the hand down until his fingers slipped around hers. "Good-bye, Sar."

Suddenly, Sarah moved and Will put his arms around her, and they stood silent, the only motion her fingers circling in the curls above his collar.

He left them. Down the trail, past the house, until Dan couldn't see the white of his shirt or hear the echoes of his shoes on the loose rocks of the trail.

Sarah left a while later. She'd asked him if he needed help, but he said no, he'd be in soon.

Right now he wanted to keep the darkness around him for a while longer.

Tomorrow Will would climb on that airplane to California.

He took a breath, feeling his head lighten.

For the first time in his life he didn't know what he'd be doing tomorrow.

That was OK.

No matter how hard it got, it would be OK.

He'd been there before, all those times, sitting in the door of a plane, above a morning sky, foolish enough to trust the cold blue wind to carry him.

Only difference was, this one he'd do alone.